CASINO EXCELSIOR

GRAHAM TEMPEST

BRIGHTWAY PRESS

Oliver Steele and Kon Feaver thrillers:

CASINO EXCELSIOR
Brightway Press, 522 Hunt Club Blvd., Apopka, Florida 32703
ISBN (Print): 978-0-9996727-0-9, bp#260520a

"'One man's terrorist is another man's freedom fighter.' That's a catchy phrase, but also misleading. Freedom fighters do not need to terrorise a population into submission."

RONALD REAGAN

1

The terrorist known as the Camel was fine-tuning his plan to blow up a planeload of Christian missionaries on the island of Mindanao in the Philippines.

It was an ambitious project, but the Camel was more than equal to the task. He had masterminded the kidnapping and beheading of three U.S. missionaries on Mindanao a few years earlier.

Nobody who knew his history could doubt that he was well able to deliver chaos again.

2

Bring me something to drink!"

The Camel was large and imposing. A thick black beard concealed the jutting chin and full lips that inspired his nickname when he was a student at Berkeley twenty years ago. He projected an air of massive weariness but the weariness masked intense religious zeal.

He was standing outside a camouflaged tent in the jungle camp of the Abu Saif Muslim separatists on the island of Basilan just west of Mindanao. His servant Ramon brought him a tin cup of tuba, the alcoholic drink made from the sap of the lauan tree.

"What's our cash position?" he growled at Kanoo, his book keeper.

"We have enough to support ourselves for several months."

"But not to pay for the hardware?"

"Alas no."

The Camel shrugged. Despite the lack of cash he was feeling optimistic. His planning was complete and he was ready to destroy the 'plane carrying the delegation of the United Missionaries in Christ as they landed at Cebu airport in two weeks' time. But he needed enough money to secure two Exocet missiles that were stored in bond down at the port. Payment was required to release them.

He looked at his watch – it was mid-morning. He walked into his tent. It was time to call Saddiq, his cash connection in Las Vegas.

The prospect of talking to Saddiq always put the Camel in a bad mood, but he had to have money. He had never met Saddiq, one of the regional paymasters for Al Qaeda scattered around the world, but the jerky image when they spoke on Skype told him all he needed to know.

Saddiq was a swarthy, fast-talking young computer salesman, fond of gold jewellery and hand-made suits from Rodeo Drive. He sweated a lot, button eyes flickering as he talked and could not resist trying to screw his adversaries. How in Satan's name had someone so worthless come to hold the Camel's destiny in his hands? In fact, Saddiq owed his position to his father, a prosperous Algerian building contractor and a secret supporter of Al Qaeda in North Africa.

The Camel was convinced that Saddiq had funds available. Saddiq denied this. "It's difficult to find donors these days. Frankly, they are all scared. Homeland Security is looking into many of the charities we used to use as conduits. What can I do?"

But today, he sounded more accommodating. "I have a line on some money."

"How much, and when?"

Saddiq hesitated. He hated sharing information. "In six figures," he said. "Low six figures," he added. He did not want the Camel to get ideas.

"When?"

"Shortly."

"Within a week?"

"Perhaps."

"Call me when it happens." The Camel believed nothing Saddiq said.

"Sure, buddy." Saddiq flashed his slick salesman's smile and ended the call.

The Camel sighed. He strongly suspected Saddiq of skimming off a hefty share of the funds passing through his hands. But there was no money in the Philippines, at least not for the Camel. There were rich Filipinos but none sympathetic to his cause, they were mostly among the charmed circle of friends of the Marcos regime.

Ramon hovered, his timid smile enquiring, his smooth brown body wrapped in a flowered sarong. He met the Camel's eye and looked down modestly.

"I am coming, child," muttered the Camel. He hauled himself heavily to his feet. He would deal with his problems tomorrow when he felt fresh.

IN LAS VEGAS, Saddiq needed to think. He was desperate to find money, but not just for the Camel. Pressure was coming from another direction.

He moved money around the world disguised as payment for computers. He always made sure that he was not personally out of pocket by taking a percentage as the money flowed by. But recently a young Saudi royal, an accountant in London, had been studying the group's cash flow. Saddiq was asked to explain $10 million that was unaccounted for. The princeling suggested that Saddiq had helped himself to the money.

Which he had, of course. You didn't do that kind of work for nothing. He was taking big risks. Surely they understood? But apparently they did not. He was told that unless he made good the shortfall his life would not be worth very much.

He was working on a source that would bail him out of trouble – funds embezzled by the late President Marcos. Saddiq's wife and her friends were from the Philippines, where the subject was common knowledge. Listening to them talk, Saddiq had taken to wondering how he could personally annex some of that 'Marcos money.' It would not be easy – people who controlled millions tended to guard them fiercely – but he had some thoughts on the subject.

3

K now what I think?" Carlton Tisch frowned round the baccarat table. "One of you four had Kalestian killed, to cheat the rest of us. If so whoever it was will regret it!"

Tisch was a wiry New Yorker, grey-haired and with the suntan of a frequent sailor. He and the other wealthy gamblers at the table were all unhappy. They had just learned that the $2 million each had contributed as ante for The Game was lost. They had given the money to casino owner Ara Kalestian and Ara was dead, gunned down yesterday in Los Angeles.

Publisher Sidney Baxter, three hundred pounds, with a red face and massive belly, frowned. When he spoke, his rumbling English voice was calm.

"I was five thousand miles away on my yacht in

Monte Carlo when Ara died. Where were you, Carlton?" He raised bushy eyebrows and smiled at Tisch without humor. Their eyes met and held. One stare from Tisch's piercing blue eyes was normally enough to stop a grizzly in its tracks but Baxter, whose ego matched his huge size, was unmoved.

"I doubt if anyone here actually pulled the trigger," said the Honorable Quentin Teague blinking through thick spectacles. A solidly built young man with a plain face and rimless glasses, he wore a grey pinstripe suit, lightweight in the desert heat. Unlike Baxter who hailed from somewhere in central Europe, he really was English. In his early thirties, he was the eldest son of the ninth Baron Teague of Hambleden, but he was self-made financially. His mild manner belied an insatiable appetite for corporate takeovers, making him, on paper, the wealthiest person at the table.

"We must look forward gentlemen, not back," said Dr Louise Chang from Hong Kong.

Elegant at 75, she was the doyenne of the group. She controlled a fleet of tankers weighing five million tons. It was managed by three of her sons, giving her time to enjoy her passion – gambling – to the full.

She turned to their host. "What do you think, Michael? Is the prize still out there?"

Michael, the dead man's son, nodded energetically. "You bet it is." A black-moustached young Armenian-American with a weightlifter's chest, he did not appear too devastated by Ara's death.

"The man who shot my father was apparently a hit man, a professional killer. The police have some leads, but they do not sound very confident. However, he was well advanced with your project and, I would say, close to success."

"As long as there's a chance, I suppose we should keep things going," grumbled Tisch, having failed to intimidate any of his colleagues.

Dr Chang nodded. To her, like the others around the table, this was just another gamble, albeit a large one.

"My thought too," she smiled.

4

Louise Chang found herself going down in the elevator with Sidney Baxter. There was barely room in the paneled cubicle for the two of them. She was not small – five foot six, slim and erect – but Baxter towered over her, a bulky six foot four and extrovert in every way. From his perfect teeth and suspiciously black hair to a Rolex the size of Big Ben, everything about him glistened.

"What do you make of young Kalestian?" he boomed. He leaned forward until their faces were inches apart and tapped her shoulder.

Her smile did not alter by a millimeter but even to Baxter it was clear the contact was unwelcome. Louise had developed a certain serenity as she grew older but she had seen plenty of the rough side of life. Coming up in Hong Kong when the levers of power were still in the hands of the British, she had prospered thanks to iron nerves, surviving physical danger and intimidation.

"Seems a nice young man," she said.

Baxter snorted. "Inexperienced. Doubt if he knows an anstalt from a stiftung."

Louise had used both business entities as ways to shelter her wealth from the Chinese when they retrieved Hong Kong from the British, but she contrived to look baffled. Baxter blundered on.

"Where do you think the money is?"

She raised her eyebrows. "Which money?"

"My two million. And yours."

"Probably spent and gone."

He almost exploded. "You take it very casually."

"Not really the point, is it?"

"Meaning?"

"The real prize is far bigger, more like four hundred million."

"What makes you think the four hundred is not 'spent and gone' as well?"

"Just a feeling."

Baxter frowned. He had a feeling, too, a feeling of uncertainty. He desperately needed to get his hands on some of that money. If Louise Chang knew where it was, that was something Baxter wanted to know.

"We should collaborate," he said abruptly.

"We?"

"You and I."

"What about our partners?"

Baxter smirked uncertainly.

The elevator came to a smooth halt.

"Well here we are," smiled Chang. "So nice to chat like this."

The door opened and she stepped out and walked towards the street, a bit faster than normal. Baxter watched her go, not sure what to think.

5

I could feel the Bahamian sun on my back.

We had been diving off Andros from an open boat – ten fellow-divers and Captain Jack, a wiry ex-petty officer whose job between cigarettes was to make sure none of us did anything really stupid. We had spent half an hour seventy feet down and I was pleasantly tired. I was not pleased when Roley the deck hand told me there was a call from Carlton Tisch.

"You want to call him back? The signal is kind of weak."

"Where was he calling from?"

"Didn't say."

"I'll call him from the lodge."

"He said it was urgent."

"Everything's urgent with him."

Roley shrugged.

Tisch had done it again – spoiled my serenity early in the day.

I tried to put it out of my mind.

CAPTAIN JACK WAS PREPARING us for the afternoon dive.

"We'll be 110 feet down. Avoid the caves, the rock is sharp and the current can get strong. If you stray into it you can get swept away."

There was nodding, but not from a couple called Donald and Wendy. Grumpy-faced Donald looked like inherited money. Wendy wore a great tan and an orange bikini but she was a novice diver. They were bickering about something.

My diving buddy was Sam, a doctor from Chicago. We let out air and sank for a hundred feet before slowing. At this depth all was shades of blue. We admired two giant clams – primitive life forms thirty inches across and a hundred years old, their fluted shells half open. I saw a flash of orange as Wendy swam towards the caves, just where Jack had told us not to go.

Bad idea. I beckoned to Sam and we swam after her.

I felt a disorienting tug as the scenery started drifting and we had to swim as hard as we could just to keep stationary. Then we were round the corner, out of sight of the others.

Of Wendy, no sign.

I was close to one of the caves. It looked scary, a jagged opening. Would she go inside after being warned not to?

I eased my way inside – the rocks were razor sharp.

At first she was nowhere in sight, but then I looked up and saw her.

Her body was pressed against the rocky ceiling, limbs moving feebly. When I got closer I saw her air hose was torn. Bubbles streamed from the line.

Scuba apparatus includes a back-up breathing line. I kicked up, unhooked her back-up mouthpiece and thrust it between her lips. Nothing happened. Her pressure gauge told me why – she was out of air, probably due to thrashing about in a panic.

There was another option. I could give her my own backup. For that I would have to get closer. A terrified novice, out of air and scared of drowning, was a major hazard. I could have my own mouthpiece ripped away. But I had to try. I tapped her mask.

Her eyes swiveled towards me, pupils dilated. She grabbed my throat. I wrenched her arm away, pulled my backup from its Velcro restraint and jammed it into her mouth.

She choked, spewing bubbles. At least she was breathing, but at the expense of my own air supply, now depleting fast. I got an arm round her waist and kicked towards the mouth of the cave. She had the sense not to resist but I grazed my arm from wrist to elbow, a black cloud of blood spreading.

Then we were out, the current sweeping us away. I've never been as relieved as when Captain Jack deftly substituted his own mouthpiece for mine. He and Sam grabbed Wendy's arms and manhandled her to safety. I followed, near exhaustion.

Roley pulled us into the boat and gave Wendy oxygen from an emergency cylinder. She promptly fell asleep.

On the ride home, Jack unlocked the cooler and handed round Budweisers. He said little but his expression spoke volumes.

6

W hen I was ready to talk to Tisch, I strolled over to the office.

Nobody would mistake Casa Bertram for a luxury hotel. The a/c units vibrated badly and you had to choose between too hot or too noisy. The decor was varnished sailfish and kitschy shell patterns, but it had a good dive shop and divemasters who knew the reef backwards. Madame Bertram logged onto the internet so that I could call Tisch on Skype.

"You took your time," he barked.

"What do you want?" It may sound rude to take that tone with a senior businessman, but it was the only way with Tisch.

"I need you here. I'm in Las Vegas."

I calculated quickly. Today was Wednesday. Tomorrow, Jack had promised to introduce us to a conger eel called Waldo that lived in a wreck off the leeward shore.

"I could be there on Saturday."

"Not Saturday. Today."

"This isn't Los Angeles, Carlton. I'm on an island in the Bahamas. The last flight just left.

"Take the ferry."

Tisch knew the Caribbean. Besides airplanes, there's usually an old-fashioned steamer that chugs along at twelve knots carrying islanders and their livestock.

"It leaves any minute."

"Better hurry, then."

"What's this about?"

"Tell you when I see you."

"Not good enough. If you want me to give up two diving days, I need more."

I held my breath. He was my biggest client. He owned the house in Los Angeles where I lived rent-free, a gilded cage.

"A man I invested money with has died."

"Sorry to hear it. I can't bring him back though."

"I want my money."

There it was. He loathed losing money. He had got rich by watching every penny. Misplacing a dollar bill caused him serious pain.

"Where's the money now?"

"I don't know."

That was an admission. His usual mode was to keep a tight hold on the purse strings. I pictured the small, terrier-like man mortified at having lost control of a substantial slice of his own money.

"Who's dead?"

"Ara Kalestian."

"The owner of the Excelsior?"

"Yes."

Ara Kalestian was another billionaire, much higher-profile than Tisch whose own successes were kept carefully low key, away from the public eye. It helped explain why Tisch had lost control of his money – someone as big as Kalestian might not stand for the sort of tight oversight Tisch usually exerted.

"How much did you give him?"

"Two million."

"For what?"

"You don't need to know."

"Yes, I do."

More dead air. I tried again.

"How did he die?"

"He was shot while leaving a building in Los Angeles."

"Do they know who did it?"

"No." Tisch sounded grumpy. He had a short

attention span at the best of times. I was becoming intrigued, so I capitulated.

"I want to fly first class," I said.

"That's not necessary."

My turn to get irritated. "I'm facing a tedious overnight boat trip. Then a nine hour flight from Nassau to Las Vegas, changing in Miami which is not exactly a fun airport."

"Okay, but use your frequent flier miles."

What a cheapskate.

IN LAS VEGAS, Saddiq had tapped Carlton Tisch's telephone. In a windowless office over a drab computer store in north Vegas, he listened to Oliver's call. When it ended, he took off his headphones, thought for a minute and then made a call of his own to a Miami number.

I WAS in a tearing hurry to catch the ferry, with barely ten minutes to pack and hustle down to the jetty. I went into 'open the bag and throw everything in' mode, and started throwing.

7

Carlton Tisch was un-trusting by nature. After speaking to Oliver, he made two more calls.

The first was to Kathy Smith, a young woman in Fort Lauderdale. Kathy, 25, blonde and wholesome, was a tennis partner of his wife Mimi. She was also a CPA with a non-linear mind, adept at tracking international movements of money.

They talked. Later that day she would take a cab from her home to the sprawling mess that was Fort Lauderdale Airport and board a flight for California.

The other call was to his friend Kon Feaver in the Florida Keys.

It was hot in the Keys as usual. The burly Israeli was out on his deck with a rod and line, trying to catch something for supper.

"It's Carlton."

"What's up?"

"Got a problem."

Having known each other for years, the minimum words sufficed. They were complementary personalities, both of them shrewd but in contrasting ways. Feaver, physically tough and a natural athlete, was not a financial person, in fact he was permanently broke. Carlton Tisch used him as a surrogate in situations where he did not wish to be liable himself. Feaver sat on the boards of several companies controlled by Carlton.

"Things are getting out of hand."

"I read where Ara Kalestian got himself shot," said Kon. "You didn't have anything to do with that, did you?"

"Of course not,"

Not that it mattered to Kon. Little shocked him. His career had been checkered. As a young man, he had played professional soccer. He was drafted into the Israeli Air Force and qualified as a fighter pilot before being grounded for chronic drunkenness. Sobering up, he kicked around the world, spent time as a mercenary in West Africa and then a few months dealing weed in Miami before deciding that the unsavory company outweighed the rewards. He got in touch with Tisch, who knew Kon's father and lived on Tortola. The New Yorker hired the son to look after his boat, and they formed a bond.

"Vegas is too noisy," said Carlton. "I want to get back to Tortola, but there's some heavy stuff going on. I need someone here I can rely on."

"What about Oliver Steele?"

Tisch shrugged. "Energetic, but he has rough edges."

Feaver translated that as 'He has the cheek to disagree with me.' Feaver disagreed with Carlton too but he did it with a Levantine obliqueness that was more effective.

"No problem," he said.

Coquina Key suited Kon. A hundred miles south of Miami, it was so small it barely existed. Occasionally, when a hurricane threatened he had to leave in a hurry but otherwise life was pretty quiet. The fishing was great. His cabin, built of concrete blocks, was plain but sturdy, with its own generator. A camouflaged hangar housed the amphibious de Havilland Beaver in which he could reach most of the Caribbean in a few hours.

At dawn next day, he released the plane from its moorings and taxied into open water, accelerated along a path parallel to US1, the highway running the length of the Keys, and flew north.

He would park at Opa-locka Executive airport,

take a taxi ten miles down the road to Miami International and catch a commercial flight. Tisch was assembling his troops.

8

As Oliver was changing planes in Miami, he was watched by a man in his thirties, inconspicuous in white short-sleeved shirt and dark trousers. The man followed Oliver to the departure gate and boarded the same flight. He sat in economy but got up somewhere over New Mexico to check that Oliver was still in first-class. He confirmed this to his satisfaction before the stewardess shooed him back to his seat.

9

I ordered a split of champagne at Carlton's expense and reached Las Vegas rested and feeling no pain.

He had a suite, and not just any old suite. It was a two-story town house twice the size of my place in Santa Monica, sitting on the flat roof of the Excelsior resort. Access was by elevator with a coded keycard. The marble floor was strewn with Persian rugs. Huge windows looked down on the Strip.

I eyed a Matisse lithograph. "Nice digs."

"It's okay."

"So what's the fuss about?"

He handed me a business card. I studied it. "Murray Segal, CPA. Is he of interest?"

"He's Ara Kalestian's accountant."

"And?"

"Kalestian was shot as he was leaving Segal's office last Saturday, as you would know if you read the news."

"I've been diving. Did Segal shoot him?"

"I doubt it, but you had better ask Segal."

"Did you think to ask him yourself?"

Tisch shrugged. "I'm old and getting tired."

He uses that line a lot. He's a hyperactive sixty. Wife number three, Mimi is twenty-five.

"I'm not too fresh myself, after twenty-four hours traveling."

"My heart bleeds." He glanced at his watch, the diamond-encrusted pride of a famous Swiss firm that advertises lavishly in the New York Times. "There are still flights to L.A. tonight. You can visit him first thing tomorrow."

We'll see, I thought.

10

I did fly out that evening. No reason to overnight in Vegas unless you're a gambler. I don't gamble much, for the same reason I don't smoke or do drugs – too expensive. I've tried them all and the kick is okay but, in my view, not worth the money.

And Tisch *is* my boss, at least for now.

It was midnight when I got to Santa Monica. My lodger Magda was asleep. Magda is Serbian, blonde and handsome, a heavier Grace Kelly who drives a red Mazda sports car. Her IQ is off the scale but she doesn't like to work – she freelances for the Sand Institute, a Malibu think-tank. She's into lesbian politics and is always out at some meeting or other, which makes our relationship nice and straightforward. I found half a pizza in the fridge, pepperoni with anchovy, nuked it, ate it, and went to bed.

In the morning, rather than barge in on Segal and risk rejection, I called his office and made an appointment. I said I needed a tax return. I put together some numbers and e-mailed them to him. The following day I visited him in Encino, check book in hand.

We shook hands and I sat down.

Segal was 50, pale and fleshy, bald on top. He wore a short-sleeved white shirt and no tie, white undershirt showing at the neck. No plastic pocket protector but you expected one, he looked like the accountant in a movie. Studio City was just up the road so maybe the image was supposed to impress his clients in the industry. I had asked around and learned he was apt to get testy during tax season. He prepared a thousand returns between January and April. He never broke the law outright but took aggressive positions in the grey areas.

He pushed papers across the desk. There was a Federal return, a California return, and a bill.

"Sign!" He tapped the returns with a stubby finger.

I signed. He signed them himself and stuffed them in two pre-addressed envelopes for me to mail. The bill was four hundred dollars. I wrote a check.

He put it in a drawer, rolled his eyes, and leaned back in his chair.

"What else do you want to know?"

I raised my eyebrows.

"Let's not waste time. You're here about Kalestian."

"Am I?"

"You say you're an accountant. You could have prepared those returns yourself. Probably already done so."

Pointless to deny. "Do you want to know why I'm really here?"

"Not really. If you want to piss away four C's to satisfy your curiosity, good luck. A lot of folk have been sniffing around, journalists, police, whatever. I hope your check will clear, by the way."

"It will. Tell me about Kalestian."

"He was worth a lot of money."

"How much is a lot?"

"It's in Forbes, you can look it up."

"So how much?"

"Twelve billion."

"That's a lot. Real estate?"

"Originally. He also owned one of the biggest casinos in Las Vegas."

"Did he make his money recently?"

"No." Segal took a deep breath and stretched in

his chair. Like a lot of people whose dull lives suddenly turn dramatic he was happy to talk.

"In 1917, while the Turks were killing Armenians, Ara's grandparents fled to California and planted olive trees. Ara grew up farming. Then he bought a patch of land in Northern California and developed it. It was plumb in the centre of what is now Silicon Valley."

"Smart move."

"Smart guy."

What happened last week?"

"He came in about his taxes, which are compli-cated. All the elements: dividends, capital gains, partnerships. Lots of partnerships."

"How many?"

"More than a hundred."

I was surprised that a big time developer would take his business to someone like Murray, tax preparer to Hollywood's B-list. He read my mind. "I've been doing the family's taxes forever."

"How long was he here?"

"An hour. When he left, I decided to grab some fresh air. As I opened the door to the stairs, I heard a noise like a champagne cork popping but I thought nothing of it.

I walked down one flight. Kalestian was lying on the landing. A man was crouched over his body. He straightened up. We made eye contact. He was neatly dressed – suit and tie. A shiny object in his hand. He pointed it at me and, frankly, I shut my eyes. I sensed a flash. I stumbled and twisted my ankle. It hurt. I thought, is this what it's like to die?"

"But you weren't dead?"

"I had been photographed, not shot. The shiny object was a camera."

"A camera?"

"What can I tell you?"

"Sorry. Go on."

"When I opened my eyes, he was gone. I limped down to the street, but all I could see was a dark blue Mercedes with tinted windows and mud all over the rear plate. It ran a red light at Coldwater Canyon and kept going."

"Why didn't you follow him?"

Segal shrugged. "Waste of time. It was a hundred degrees outside. My car was in the underground park. Ventura Boulevard is many miles long. I went back."

"To the stairs?"

"To the body. Even to my inexpert eye, Kalestian was dead. He was on his back. A pool of blood the size of a beer coaster on his chest. He was holding the envelope I had given him. I put my ear to his mouth. Nothing."

"What did you do?"

"Left him to his eternal rest and went upstairs."

I would have done much the same, I thought.

"You called the police?"

Segal nodded. "They asked a lot of questions. Apparently I was credible. Beyond our professional relationship, Kalestian and I were strangers. I've never been to his house."

"You used your 'I'm busy, who do I bill for my time' manner?"

He smiled drily. "CPAs have a license to be brusque."

"Then what?"

"Yellow tape. Technicians. The body taken away. Normal day for the police, I suppose."

I got up. "Thanks for your help, Mr. Segal."

"Thanks for your business."

As I left, he opened another file and turned back to his computer.

BACK IN MY CAR – yellow 1970 Mustang, rag top:

It was almost noon. There was an In-N-Out Burger in nearby Woodland Hills. The Mustang took me there of its own accord. Sitting in the sun, working on a Double Double and a strawberry shake, it was easier to think.

Segal hadn't been much help. I now knew that the killer wore a suit and tie, which sure narrowed things down. Some useful background on Kalestian, but I was no closer to finding Carlton's money.

Come to think, what was I looking for – Carlton's $2 million or Kalestian's killer? Answer: Tisch was paying me to find the money. Nobody was paying me to solve a murder.

But the two had to be related. I would pursue both. Problem solved. That Double Double usually does the trick.

11

I wondered what the police were up to.

So I went to Van Nuys police station. I spoke to someone called Detective Pedro Gray. I disliked him on sight. He was pale and thin, maybe forty, receding chin and prominent Adam's apple. Black-rimmed specs on a bony nose. No smile.

We exchanged cards. He studied mine.

"Steele Investments, Oliver Steele, President." He subtly conveyed the thought that I was an impostor. "What can I do for you, Oliver?"

I hate it when strangers use my first name, especially strangers in authority. To retaliate I called him Pedro, rather than 'Detective.' He blinked but took it in stride, making me feel foolish.

I asked, "Pedro, bring me up to date regarding the murder of Ara Kalestian."

"Why should I do that?"

"Why not? I'm retained by one of his partners."

He frowned. I sensed a brick wall looming. I pulled out my mobile and called Carlton.

"Tisch." Impatient as usual.

"I need you to call Michael Kalestian and have him phone this detective." I read off the name and phone number on Gray's card. "He needs to vouch for me, so that I can get some co-operation."

"Leave it with me."

Two minutes later, Gray's mobile rang. He listened, rang off and frowned. "What do you need?"

"Whatever you have."

It wasn't much. Mostly what Segal had already told me. Not worth antagonizing the police for.

Our parting was frosty.

THE AIR above the roadway shimmered as I took the Sepulveda Pass south through the Santa Monica mountains.

Los Angeles is dry and dusty most of the time but when it rains, as it had the day before, the raindrops scrub the air and make the whole basin seem smaller. From downtown you can see the Hollywood Hills and, to the south, the slopes of Palos Verdes.

Due west was Santa Monica, my home town, one

of a series of beach communities along Pacific Coast Highway.

The beach culture is strong. Pulling off the freeway at Santa Monica Boulevard, I overtook a battered truck barely firing on three cylinders, surf-board in the back, stereo throbbing. The driver, a tanned kid in reflectors, looked like me ten years ago.

I pulled into my driveway. The 1940s ranch-style house was a block from the beach. Not much to look at but, because of where it was, a couple of million of anyone's money – in this case Carlton's. At the back, a pool and a strip of lawn and on the far wall a gnarled vine, dusted with tiny grapes.

Magda was in the kitchen.

"Waffles?"

"Brilliant."

She frowned. "Sometimes you sound like a British character actor." She could do a perfect British accent when she chose.

"Nothing wrong with being a British actor in L.A. They make a good living."

She wrinkled her nose. But it got me thinking. I had been here a year – living at the beach, driving the Mustang. Was I getting too old for all that?

No. My only fault was an addiction to sunshine. Yes I hung out at the beach while others were tack-ling steady jobs, but so what?

Six months ago I invested a small inheritance in developing a four unit apartment building in Venice. One of Southern California's periodic real estate booms was in progress, so the timing was good. Three units were already sold. I called my builder, Clyde.

He was doing fine without me so I set to work on Magda's waffles. Then I went for a swim. Then I lay by the pool. The temperature hit 101. In the evening, Magda and I had supper at Fritto Misto on Colorado, my favorite Italian.

THE MAN from Miami had been shadowing Oliver for several days. He hadn't made it to a laundromat and his shirt was getting itchy.

He had a Chevy truck rented from Thrifty. He waited outside Murray Segal's office while Oliver was there. He followed him to Inn-N-Out Burger. Then he trailed him to Santa Monica. Once he was sure Oliver was home for the day he drove a few hundred yards, parked and phoned Saddiq, speaking Arabic.

12

N ext morning, my phone rang.

"Mr Steele?" The woman's voice had an Indian lilt. "This is Dr Advani at Cedars Sinai, calling on behalf of Murray Segal."

"Yes?"

"Mr. Segal has been admitted with head injuries. He arrived in a coma. He's conscious now, but in intensive care. He asked to see you."

"I'll come round."

"Take your time," she said. "He won't be leaving today."

MURRAY SEGAL WAS PROPPED up in bed. An oxygen tube crossed his face beneath his nose and an i-v line dripped fluid into his arm.

"What happened?"

"I was mugged."

Between sniffs of oxygen, he told the story.

"I got to work around 8am. The place was a mess – filing cabinets forced open, papers on the floor."

"And?"

"Someone was behind the door." He grimaced. "My skull feels as if it had been split with an axe."

"It almost was," said Dr Advani. "He was hit as hard as someone can be hit and still survive." Her black hair hung in a long plait over white-coated shoulders. "Another five minutes and he would not be talking to us."

He tried to smile. "I must have an extra layer of bone."

"Was it just one man?" I asked.

"I guess so."

"What did he take?"

"Tax returns."

"Any idea why?"

"No."

"Well, there must be a link with Ara Kalestian."

Agreement flickered across Murray's brow, then faded. He was either tired or uneasy.

"He needs sleep." Dr Advani tried to shepherd me away, but I sensed Murray wanted to say something.

"Which returns were taken, Murray?"

"Several."

"Was one of them Kalestian's?"

"Yes."

The doctor was closing in. I had a thought.

"Are you the only person who knew Kalestian's whole financial situation?"

"I guess so. Some things he did not share even with me."

"Such as?"

"Casino stuff. The Excelsior."

The Excelsior was in the middle of the Strip. It was a favorite of high rollers, gamblers who risked thousands on a single card. If you bet in the millions, the Excelsior was one of a handful of casinos that would wine and dine you within an inch of your life if that's what it took to coax you into their elegant rooms.

"Did he own the Excelsior outright?"

"Forty per cent. There were other, lesser partners."

"Who inherits?"

"His wife for her lifetime. Then it gets complicated. There are trusts."

"Time to go," said the doctor. Murray raised a hand.

"There's a question you didn't ask."

"What's that?"

"Besides Kalestian, whose return was taken?"

"Whose?"

"Yours," said Murray.

13

Driving home, I began to worry.

Murray had warned me. Whoever raided his office – likely Kalestian's killer – now knew my address. Handy if his next assignment should be me.

But if I *was* a target, why?

Then I remembered the manila envelope Kalestian was carrying when he was shot. Where was it? What was in it? The killer might wonder if I had read its contents myself.

I still had Detective Gray's card. I dialed the number.

"Pedro?"

"Speaking."

"Oliver Steele. I came to see you about Ara Kalestian."

"Yes, Oliver?" Not hostile but not friendly either.

"Did you know Murray Segal was attacked and is in hospital?"

"Yes, we know."

"Documents were stolen, including my personal tax return."

Silence again.

"Whoever mugged Segal was looking for something. Posibly that manila envelope Kalestian was carrying. They may think I have it."

"Is that so?"

"I assume you have it. What's in it?"

"I can't say."

"Will it be followed up?"

"Yes."

"But you haven't done so yet?"

"You can leave it to us, Mr. Steele." At least he had stopped calling me Oliver.

"If I knew what was in it, maybe I could help."

"If we think so we'll let you know."

Well, screw that. I was not going to wait on the sidelines. I called Cedars Sinai and asked for Murray.

He said he felt better.

"What was in the manila envelope, Murray?"

"That's confidential."

"But Kalestian is dead."

"It's confidential to his estate."

"Then I need to talk to his estate."

"That would be his widow."

"When can I see her?"

"I don't know."

I began to get irritated. "Why won't you help?"

Silence.

"If I'm murdered it will be your fault."

"I suppose you could talk to my secretary," Murray said wearily.

14

I spoke to Murray's secretary, Janice. She was a tower of strength. She had been with Murray forever and when she took a hand, things got done. She arranged for me to visit Kalestian's widow at the family home near Fresno.

"A word of advice," she said, "Modesta Kalestian is old school – respectable, religious. She'll like your accent, but you must mind your Ps and Qs."

"Got it."

"I told her you are an inheritance tax expert."

"Oh really?"

"You are going there to begin listing the estate's assets. It's something Murray will need."

"Murray's okay with that?"

She shrugged. "You need a cover story."

She couriered me Kalestian's bulky tax return and directions for the three-hour drive.

I WAS SORTING papers for the trip when the phone rang.

"It's Kathy."

My heart sank. My life was about to become unmanageable. But I also came pleasantly awake. In the Casino Caribbean affair Kathy Smith turned out, after a rocky start, to be my saviour as well as a mental sparring partner. Afterwards, we spent a week on a live-aboard dive boat. I had a vague idea of not wanting to mix business with pleasure, but that was before she came into my cabin, stripped off her wet bathing suit and helped me do the same.

"Where are you?"

"Heading your way. I'll be there tonight."

"Why?"

"Carlton called me."

"Did he tell you about Kalestian?"

"Yep."

"Did he call you, or vice versa?"

"He called me."

"Doesn't he trust me to fix this?" I hoped I was concealing any resentment.

"Maybe he thought two heads were better than

one." She had a master's degree in international tax from USC. "He comped me a first-class ticket."

"Business class?"

"First class."

"Did you ask for that?"

"No, he offered."

THAT EVENING, in a bad mood, I met her at LAX and we drove back to Santa Monica. It's hard to be upset with Kathy for long, she's too darned cheerful.

We were lying together under a light duvet a few hours later when there was a knock and the bedroom door opened. Magda stood there smiling in a crisp white pajama top whose hem reached her tanned hips.

"Room for one more under there?"

Kathy looked at me and I shrugged. She rolled her eyes.

NEXT MORNING I got up early to drive to Fresno. I was making coffee when Kathy appeared.

"Magda's fun but I don't think I'll stay. One can have too much of a good thing."

"I agree." It had been an exhausting evening.

I dropped her off at Shutters, an expensive hotel

down at the beach. There are some perks to working for a billionaire.

"Got any plans?" I asked.

"Think I'll snoop around. Might go to Vegas," was all she would say.

15

Saddiq was talking to the Camel.

"There's a guy in LA who may cause problems," said Saddiq. "I have a line on the money, but this jerk is threatening to chisel in ahead of me."

"Who is he?"

"Name of Steele."

"What do you know about him?"

"British, lives in Santa Monica. Fancies himself as an athlete – squash, diving, that kind of thing. I need to check him out, but he doesn't sound a real threat."

The big Filipino stared at Saddiq's image. "You never know."

He did not feel comfortable working through Saddiq. He wondered if the man had the mental toughness to take care of folk like Steele. The Camel had contacts in California from his student days but there were reasons he did not want to use them. If a second death was linked to Kalestian, a media blizzard would follow. That could be disastrous.

16

My route to Fresno took me north past Bakersfield. As I passed mile upon mile of open field, I had time to think.

So the widow was religious. That gave me an idea of what to expect. California is home to a huge array of religions and the San Joaquin Valley is no exception. The Kalestians were Armenian Christians. I get uneasy when I'm faced with someone of strong faith like this woman, so I could be in for an awkward time.

I stopped for gas in a small town twenty miles south of Fresno – a few shacks under an open sky, in endlessly flat country. Disciplined orchards alternated with infinite fields of what looked like spinach. Laborers in sombreros bent over their hoes.

A movie theatre advertised its program in dusty Spanish.

Fresno is the largest city in the San Joaquin Valley. Mid way between Los Angeles and San Francisco, the valley is the main agricultural area in California, the world's fifth largest supplier of food. Agriculture is dominated by big corporations nowadays, but there are still some major farming families including, as I would learn, the Kalestians.

ACCESS to the property lay through massive wrought-iron gates. I had to identify myself before being allowed in. I drove for another mile through lemon orchards, tart scent wafting through the car, before the road forked and a sign pointed me to the house.

The Kalestian home was arranged around three sides of a courtyard. It was built in the French Empire style and immaculately maintained. The courtyard was deserted. A fountain played, steaming in the heat. A flame-red Corvette stood in the shade of a eucalyptus tree.

Double doors gleamed with brass fittings. They opened before I could ring the bell and a grey-clad maid ushered me in. A long dark hallway led to a sitting room at the back of the house. I was asked to wait.

Outside, well-watered lawns. Inside, a jewel-like triptych on the wall depicted bearded elders, their robes glowing with color against heavy gold leaf. Opposite, pages of illuminated text in a glass case. The characters were unfamiliar.

"Those are pages from the Divine Liturgy."

I turned. "I was trying to recognize the text."

"It's Old Armenian."

Brown eyes met mine. Modesta Kalestian was darkly handsome. Black hair with grey steaks was scraped back in an old-fashioned bun. Clearly she had been a great beauty. She wore black but I sensed this was her everyday dress, not in mourning for her husband.

She pointed to a sofa and sat beside me. "Can I offer you some iced tea?"

Something stronger would have been nice, but I accepted. "It's good of you to see me."

She nodded. She did not seem grief-stricken. I found her self-control surprising. I may have looked puzzled because she smiled.

"Did you expect me to be more affected by my husband's death?"

I said nothing, trying to be tactful.

"We led separate lives." Her gaze drifted away and then returned.

"Murray Segal says you need information. What can I tell you?"

I guess I don't have the makings of a spy, because I did not feel like lying to her. I remembered my cover story but I barreled ahead and explained why I was really there – that I had been hired to investigate the attack on her husband. She listened closely, although when I started talking about tax returns she looked a bit lost.

"Who might have wanted to harm your husband?"

She did not answer directly. "We moved in different circles. It had been that way for a while." She stared out of the window. I waited for her to gather her thoughts.

"We were married thirty years. For fifteen years, things were fine. Our children were growing up. Ara was making his mark in business. You could say our marriage was a success."

"Were you already wealthy in those days?"

"I would say comfortable."

Big house, thousands of acres – depends what you're used to, I guess.

"Ara was starting to invest in real estate. His timing was always good; everything he touched was successful."

"Then he diversified?"

She nodded. "He sold a controlling interest in the Silicon Valley property to a national developer for a lot of money. That's when the problems began."

"How so?"

"He was approached by some people who wanted to buy the Excelsior Hotel in Las Vegas. They were full of talk about how great it would be."

"They needed his money?"

"And his good name. Casino investors must be approved by the Nevada Gaming Commission and Ara's reputation was impeccable."

"Theirs were not?"

She shrugged. "They were not criminals, but they weren't good people either – too smart by half."

They probably didn't care for you either, I thought. She could be intimidating.

"I tried to get him to sell his stake. I tried many times. But he said it was a good investment, and he would stand by it."

"Who are his partners?"

"Steve Los, who owns Los Chevrolet in Bakersfield. And Gametech, an equipment group."

"Equipment?"

"Slot machines. One-armed bandits. Do you gamble, Mr. Steele?"

"Occasionally."

"I've seen many lives ruined by gambling, including some in my husband's casino."

"That must have been difficult to accept."

"It was the end of our marriage except in name. I could no longer respect Ara. Even worse, my son

Michael sided with him. He became a vice-president at the casino."

I stared out of the window. In the baking sun, a gardener in a big straw hat was trimming the already perfect hedge.

"Could one of your husband's partners be responsible for the murder?"

She shrugged. "Anything's possible."

I got up and walked over to the triptych. It was probably worth more than my annual income.

"Who benefits from your husband's death?"

"My children and myself. My son Michael is here today. He can tell you about the business side."

"How long has Michael been at the Excelsior?"

"Ever since he turned twenty-one. I did not approve. I wanted him to go into the family produce business but my husband's influence was too strong." She smiled sadly. "Harvard educated and he became a blackjack dealer."

The maid came with more tea. Modesta Kalestian said, "Clara, please ask Michael to join us." Moments later, Michael appeared.

17

In Las Vegas, Kathy Smith knocked on the door of Carlton Tisch's suite at the Excelsior. It was opened by the butler.

At least, he was dressed like a butler: black jacket, grey trousers. The face matched the trousers.

"Hi," she said. "Where's Carlton?"

"He stepped out. Who might you be?"

"Might ask you the same question." She brushed past him and looked around. The place was huge, on two floors, big picture window overlooking the Strip and a six foot high abstract dominating the foyer.

"I look after these accommodations. My name is Albert."

"Well he's supposed to meet me here, Albert."

Albert frowned as if he had the right to shield Carlton from interlopers, including young women.

But just then Carlton arrived. He was eating a Kit Kat bar from the kiosk downstairs.

"Hi, Kathy. Come into the den. Fix us some coffee, Albert."

"Yes, sir."

Kathy sensed Albert did not like being given orders – odd for a butler. She and Carlton sat down in the den.

"What's going on?" she asked.

"Oh, stuff."

Carlton had never been able to play the gruff businessman with Kathy, who was young enough to be his grand-daughter. She was the same age as Mimi, his third and apparently final wife – both women treated him with amused patience when he showed signs of getting pompous.

The truth was that the two women made him feel young again. Growing up poor on New York's lower East Side, he had enjoyed few of the carefree pleasures of youth. When rich men's sons were off at Yale or Princeton, he had found work on Wall Street but only by sweating it out in Goldman Sachs' mail-room. Those years were lost, but now he found it liberating to hang out with people much younger than himself.

So it was in a relaxed way that they chatted.

"Stuff like the murder of the guy who ran your poker game?"

"It's not poker."

"What, then?"

"Something similar."

"Where do I come in?"

"He had charge of a large pot of our money. We think he banked it offshore. I thought you could try and find it."

"How much money?"

"$8 million. I was one of four who each kicked in $2 million."

That struck her as outrageous but she knew there was no point in saying so.

A sour-looking Albert appeared, with a tray. He served coffee and then retreated, closing the door.

Kathy and Carlton talked for half an hour. Finally she said, "Last question: Oliver is working on this too. How are we supposed to interact? Who does what?"

Carlton looked flustered. It was the sort of question he hated because it called for a straight answer. His senior staff at Eastern Debt Factors had learned long ago that he was an entrepreneur, not a manager. He refused to approve an organization chart for the business. His executives muddled through using common sense and duct tape which, amazingly, seemed to work.

"Coordinate as appropriate. Keep me informed of anything significant."

A classic Tisch non-answer. She got up to leave.

When she opened the door, Albert was standing very close, polishing a brass statuette. She smiled brightly and walked straight past him.

DOWNSTAIRS, she stopped at the small food court opposite the elevator. It had a hot dog stand, a burger place and a taco stand. They looked uniformly unappealing but it was noon, so she ordered a chicken taco with guacamole and chips and went and sat by the window. Then, on a whim, she moved to a different seat, where she could watch the elevator doors, and the people emerging.

She finished her taco and was mopping up the last precious smears of guacamole when who should emerge but Albert. He did not see her but walked quickly away. She licked her fingers, got up and followed him. He walked towards the multistorey car park where he got into a dusty Toyota Corolla. In the noon rush, the Toyota took several minutes to leave the car park, a stroke of luck for Kathy. She was able to flag a passing taxi and be on the Toyota's tail as it headed north on the Strip.

They soon left the smart area and entered the seedy no-man's land between the Strip and downtown. Albert's Toyota stopped outside a computer store. She made her driver keep moving but then pull over and wait. After five minutes Albert emerged holding a carrier bag and drove off. They followed him again and this time found themselves driving out to the eastern suburbs of Las Vegas where Albert stopped, went into a modest house and stayed there. 'So what?' thought Kathy. She had the driver take her back to her hotel. But she was intrigued about the computer store. Albert had not struck her as a high-tech butler.

18

As Saddiq was having Oliver followed, he did not know that he himself was being watched from on high.

He was on the radar screen of the U.S. Treasury.

Senator Huell Ham of Nebraska, recently appointed to the Senate Anti-Terrorism Committee, was curious about the nexus between terrorism and money.

Ham was broad, overweight and chronically out of breath, not one of the workout crowd in the Senate gym. Known as 'the Hamster', he had puffy cheeks, hence his nickname, and a hunted look in front of a camera. Unlikely therefore to become president, he was able to concentrate on harvesting the many perks that come the way of a three-term senator.

He approached Jack Altman, assistant secretary for counter-terrorism. The studious Altman headed an inter-agency task force responsible for identifying the ways terrorism was financed.

"Good timing," said Altman. "We just came across something interesting."

"Namely?"

"We encourage other countries to use the same reporting rules as here in the United States."

"You mean the reporting requirement on foreign transactions over $10,000?"

"Yes. And Saudi Arabia cooperates, thanks to several visits I made to Riyadh."

"They have a similar rule?"

"Yes, although their limit is $16,000, not $10,000. I guess Arabs are just richer." He meant it as a joke but Hamster did not laugh. "Go on."

"So we found a series of transfers from Saudi individuals to a construction company in Algeria."

"And?" Ham had a short attention span.

"Algeria is a hotbed of terrorism, notably al Qaeda."

"Was this money for terrorism?"

"The donors deny it."

"What do they say it's for?"

"Building houses."

"Possibly true?"

"Unlikely. The same donors have donated to

some highly suspicious charities. Ever heard of IIRO – the International Islamic Relief Organization?"

"No."

"Or RIHS – the 'Revival of Islamic Heritage Society?'"

Ham shook his head.

"They handle both innocent and terrorist monies. It's difficult for us to identify what's illicit and what's not."

Ham looked at his watch. He had a lunch date with a female banking lobbyist.

"What use is that information?"

"By itself, not much. But we have similar lists of transfers into the United States, so we compared them. We found transfers to a man called Saddiq in Las Vegas. The Algerian company is Saddiq Construction. Look!" He pushed a page of figures towards Ham.

Ham studied it. "The sums don't match."

"Oh, they do," said Altman. "Look at the numbers in the right-hand column"

"What do they mean?"

"They are the ratios of the second payment to the first payment in each pair of transactions. Notice anything?"

"They all run around 80 per cent."

"Exactly. What does that tell you?"

"I have no idea." Ham was a politician; math was not his forté.

"It's consistent with the Algerian outfit taking a 20 per cent cut for handling the transfer. Isn't it obvious?"

Ham shook his head. "When you hear galloping, it's usually horses, not zebras." He stood up. "I have to run." Altman looked crestfallen.

Ham smiled at him. "But I like your attitude. Keep it up. Dig into that Algerian thing and keep me posted."

His driver was waiting in a black limousine.

During lunch, he thought about what he had heard. Afterwards he called the Head of the Department of Homeland Security, one of the most powerful people in Washington.

"How are you, Madam Secretary? Listen, I've been doing some research and I've found something disturbing. Yes, I'll drop by shortly."

19

Michael Kalestian burst, rather than walked, into the room. There was a cocky spring in his stride but his brown eyes looked anxious. Bushy eyebrows framed his face and his mouth was obscured by a black moustache that seemed an affectation in a young man of thirty. He pumped my hand with a bone-crushing grip.

He glanced at the triptych. "I see you've met Saints Thaddeus and Bartholomew, my mother's closest friends."

I sensed an edge in the words.

"There's a reason they look glum. When they arrived in Armenia as missionaries they were executed very unpleasantly. Later the king was converted to Christianity but by then Thad and Bart were toast."

He slapped me on the back. "Remember that, the next time you face an Armenian in a business deal."

Modesta did not look amused.

"Let's get some air," said Michael. He led the way outside.

We sat in rattan chairs on a verandah that ran the length of the house. Out in the sun, the gardener was still trimming the hedge.

"A tough life," I said.

"Isn't it though?"

"How do you handle it?"

"I keep busy." He smiled, eyes watchful. If I thought I could get him to provide information without realizing it, I could think again.

"I'm investigating your father's death."

"Why not leave that to the police?"

"The police are overworked. And I happen to be at risk personally. Your father's tax return was stolen yesterday by a party or parties unknown and, guess what, so was mine."

"Fair enough."

"Questions. First, who wanted to kill your father? Someone, clearly."

"I'd have to think."

"Is the list so long?"

"I don't have a list. I'll work on it."

"No offence, but where were you on Saturday morning, around eleven?"

A smile behind the bushy moustache. "I don't remember. I'll check. But that won't help you."

"It won't?"

"The man who pulled the trigger isn't the man you really want. It's more a matter of who gave the order, isn't it?'"

"Okay."

"Next question?"

"It's two days since your father was killed. Nobody seems prostrate with grief."

"You mean my mother? She's so spiritual I doubt if she has personal feelings for anyone. If you've talked to her you know how she felt about my dad. My sisters are devastated."

"What about you?"

"It's complicated." He looked at his watch. "I have to go to work."

I must have seemed taken aback.

"I'm not avoiding you. What are your plans?"

"To talk to you."

"Why not ride along?"

"Where to?"

"My office. I have things to do."

"Where's your office?"

"In Las Vegas."

He smiled, polite to a time-waster. In effect, 'I'll answer your questions but on my terms.'

"What about my car?" The Mustang was parked alongside the red Corvette.

"One of our drivers will take it back to L.A. He'll drop it wherever you live and come back on our truck."

Well, it was not as if I had anything better to do.

THE RED CORVETTE was Michael's. He drove aggressively back to the fork, spun in a hail of gravel and headed in the other direction. We passed long warehouses the size of aircraft hangers. Workers were loading crates of produce into eighteen-wheelers. The trucks were dark green with a logo of a silver fruit-tree and the word 'Kalestian.' Beyond the last warehouse, we stopped on the edge of emptiness, a private airfield.

A small twin-engine 'plane stood waiting. It was scarlet like the car. I don't know aircraft but it looked fast.

He disappeared into a small office. Through its glass door I watched him talk briefly, then he emerged.

"Hop in."

I gritted my teeth as he gunned the engine. Small

planes make me nervous. It just seems more accidents happen to small planes than to big ones – Buddy Holly, Rocky Marciano, it's quite a list.

The plane streaked down the runway, took off and climbed rapidly. The Kalestian mansion dwindled to the size of a Monopoly house. Michael was busy talking on the radio and trimming the plane, then he turned to me.

"Just the job for a trip across the desert."

"How fast does this thing go?"

"About two hundred."

"Leaves the 'vette standing?"

"No speed limit up here and no Highway Patrol."

Below us, tan desert stretched in all directions. The noise in the tiny cockpit made conversation difficult but Michael seemed happy to get back to the subject.

"My father was an emotional black hole. He expected unconditional love from his family and if he received anything less, he would shut you out. My sisters loved him so he treated them well. My mother was more critical, so she paid a price."

I added a piece to my picture of Ara Kalestian – selfishness.

"What about you?"

"We got on okay. I have a bit of an ego myself."

"But you went along when he sent you to dealer school."

Michael laughed. "That was no sacrifice, it was the best decision of my life. Living in Vegas, running a big casino – I enjoyed every minute. Still do!"

"What about your father's will? Who gets the Excelsior?"

"It stays in the family. My father owned 40 per cent. 25 per cent belongs to Steve Los. Gametech has another 25 per cent. The remaining 10 per cent is owned by Goldberg Freilich, the Wall Street bankers."

"For putting the deal together?"

He nodded

"Your father did not have control?"

"He could be outvoted, in theory. But it never happened."

"Who gets his shares now?"

"They are in a family trust."

"Are you a trustee?"

"Yes, along with my mother and our attorney."

"It sounds as though you just became much more powerful."

"Maybe."

"Do the other stockholders realise that?"

"I'm sure they do. You'll meet Steve Los; watch and see how he kisses up to me."

He thought for a minute. "Los and my dad had their differences. Los wants the casino to go public – sell shares to outsiders. Dad refused."

"Why did Los want that?"

"Access to money."

"Sounds reasonable."

"It is. But issuing more shares would dilute our family's ownership. We would have less control."

"How did Gametech feel?"

"They supported my father."

I changed the subject. "What's your job at the hotel?"

"I look after the invited guests."

"Invited guests?"

"The high rollers, people with big money."

"What makes someone a high roller? Where's the cutoff?"

"As they say, if you have to ask you can't afford it."

"So for instance, I would not qualify?"

He smiled. "We are at the very top end of the market. There are maybe a hundred gamblers worldwide in my target area. Many of them Chinese."

"So the Chinese really are the world's biggest gamblers?"

He nodded. "The Pacific Rim economy has created many fortunes in the four Chinas."

"Four?"

"Hong Kong, Singapore, Taiwan and Mainland China. Do you gamble?"

"Occasionally."

The most I bet on a card was ten dollars. Kalestian may have guessed that because he said: "If you normally pay your own way, this will be an experience."

A few minutes later we landed at McCarran Airport, Las Vegas.

20

At McCarran we taxied to the private terminal. A white Rolls Royce stood waiting.

The chauffeur was a sandy-haired man in his thirties, smart in a grey suit.

"Sorry about your dad, Mr. K."

"Thanks, Stephen."

The big car rode smoothly. I could not feel the road. Michael opened a walnut cabinet. From a Waterford decanter he poured us each a glass.

"Your health."

I sipped appreciatively. "Single malt, twelve years old. Is this how you treat your gamblers?"

"Only our Invited Guests."

"This car must have cost half a million."

"We have four of them."

"You're kidding!"

"No. My guests sometimes bet that much on a single card. This car paid for itself in a week."

It was the kind of money some people would kill for, I thought.

I sat back, cocooned in soft leather and watched Las Vegas unfold. Sun bounced off the glass pyramid of the Luxor Hotel. We passed the dark green MGM Grand, a leading candidate for the world's ugliest hotel. People trooped like ants through the lion's jaws that were its main entrance.

We drove north on the Strip past Caesar's Palace, famous for over-the-top luxury. Then the Mirage with its erupting volcano. Finally, leaving the dignified Bellagio on our left, we reached the Excelsior.

The star treatment began as we pulled into the forecourt.

A seven-foot porter in spotless white, beaming like a lighthouse, bowed and handed us out of the Rolls.

A chorus of greeting. "Hey Mike", "Right on Mr K.", "Good to see you Michael."

Michael smiled and pressed the flesh. The king was dead, long live the king.

"What's the plan?" I asked.

"Stick with me. We'll take the tour."

He led the way through a glass-domed conservatory housing a tropical jungle complete with palm trees, vines and brilliant flowers. I thought they were artificial until I spotted a gardener watering them.

The rattle and clang of slot machines was deafening. Finally we came to a huge atrium with banks of elevators – glass capsules that boosted residents at rocket-like speed. Michael led us straight past them to an unobtrusive door. A muscular attendant saluted and opened it to reveal yet another elevator.

"Where are we going?"

"To the exclusive area."

"Like the salle privée in Monte Carlo?"

"Except, Nevada law requires all gaming rooms be open to the public."

"So anyone can go where we're going?"

"Subject to a table limit of $10,000."

"As a maximum? That's a lot."

"As a minimum."

I got the point. I was one of the riff-raff.

The elevator rose smoothly. We stepped out into a silent world high up in the building. Wood paneling everywhere. Other signs of luxury – silk wallpaper, waxed parquet flooring, oriental rugs. Quantities of fresh flowers. Above all, silence, so rare in deafening Las Vegas, underlined that we were in the land of the rich.

"The décor is recent," said Kalestian. "You're looking at several million dollars' worth of remodeling."

I was having trouble dealing with the sums he quoted so casually. "How could it cost so much?"

"We brought the craftsmen in from France – three generations of the same family. The paneling took three months to carve. Special food airfreighted in. It adds up."

An ebony-skinned maid in a short black dress was brewing coffee in a pantry. A tuxedo-clad pit boss stood on the threshold of the card room, doing nothing. A dealer, also in tuxedo, stood in front of a single customer at the blackjack table.

So, including the dealer and the guard downstairs, four employees were being paid to wait on a single gambler. As we watched, the customer pushed back his chair.

"Everything good, Mr Baggott?" asked Michael.

"Lousy cards," the man said with an Australian twang. "Dealer's incompetent."

Kalestian's face fell. "We'll replace him tomorrow."

The man grunted. In his fifties, bald with pale blue eyes, white shirt, dark tie, he could have been a bank manager. He scowled and made for the elevator.

"Billy Baggott," said Michael softly, as if that explained everything.

"Rings a bell."

"Owns newspapers in Australia."

"Why was he sitting by himself?"

"He likes it that way."

"Doesn't sound like fun."

"It is for him. Life's a personal struggle, him against the world." Michael lowered his voice. "He's probably the least likeable person in this business."

"What's his problem?"

"Foul temper, Napoleon complex, a bully."

"But you tolerate him?"

"Not just tolerate, we give him a $20 million line of credit."

"So much?"

"He's good for it. It's less than one per cent of his net worth."

One per cent of my net worth wouldn't pay for dinner. I tried to imagine betting $10,000 on a hand. The picture wouldn't come.

Michael said, "He settles his bills on the nail, unlike some others who take a year to pay. With him we run the opposite risk – we could get over-extended if he really has a good run."

"So he's bigger than you – richer than the house?"

"And he knows it. Money does that to some people, especially new money."

He shrugged. "Enough grumbling. Let's go and meet our Chairman."

21

I 'm Steve Los." He leaped up and pumped my hand. He was barely five feet tall.

The office of the Chairman of the Board recalled the architecture of Mussolini. A blonde secretary with a 40-inch bust smiled brightly.

Los was deeply suntanned, with black hair smooth and shiny. He wore a blue suit, white shirt and the tie of a regiment I doubt he ever served in. Brown eyes flickered. His teeth were perfect, like a small beaver.

"How are ya, how are ya," he beamed. I could see why Modesta Kalestian disliked him. Ten seconds and I was exhausted.

He ushered us to a sofa and sat down opposite, the polished brogues on his little feet barely touched the floor.

A phone warbled. The secretary beckoned to Michael. "It's for you."

He spoke briefly, then turned to us.

"I must go. The Chang party is leaving. Those scoundrels at the Regency offered them unlimited credit. I have to sort it out."

Los shrugged. "Let them go."

"We'll have to match the terms."

"Don't give away the store. Maybe we can't afford to keep them."

Kalestian hurried out. Los turned to me.

"There are six Chang cousins in town. The money comes from their grandmother, Louise."

I recognized the name. She was one of Carlton's fellow Invited Guests.

"Are they big spenders?"

"Not as individuals, but they are important as a group."

He leaned forward. "I wish Michael understood how important liquidity is. We have to keep so much cash on hand. He thinks because the casino is worth a billion dollars we can write checks for that amount. We can't."

"How much could you write a check for?"

The smile grew guarded. "That depends."

"I can read it in your annual report."

Los shook his head. "Actually you can't, we're a

private company. Our balance sheet is our own business."

"It may become mine."

The beaver teeth retreated behind thin lips. "What *is* your business?"

"I'm administering Ara's estate."

"Will you be liquidating his assets?"

"Some."

"Including his Excelsior shares?"

"Everything's on the table."

His bright eyes stopped flickering round and bored into me.

"The Excelsior has to go public."

"Why?"

"Money. We need more. We have to keep pace with our competitors, companies with deep pockets. Otherwise we shall be squeezed out, become minor league players."

Our eyes met, then Los shrugged and looked away.

Michael reappeared.

"Everything okay?" Los asked.

"For now."

"What was the problem?"

"One of the cousins says there's a ghost in his room, stealing his luck. I moved him to another suite and promised to station a ghost watcher there."

Los nodded.

"You see what we are up against," said Michael. Then to me, "Let's move on."

I PROCESSED what I'd seen. Did Los rate as a suspect? He looked shifty but murder was a big step, even for someone I trusted about a millimeter. I needed more information.

"What would you like to do now?" Michael asked.

"What about your other shareholder, Gametech?"

"You want to meet them?"

"Any reason I shouldn't?"

"No. They're okay. Manufacturing folk, a bit pedestrian." He made a phone call, then turned to me.

"The man you need is out of town, getting back tonight. Breakfast tomorrow, seven thirty?"

"Fine. Can I get a room for the night?"

"I'll do better, I'll put you in a suite we keep for Invited Guests."

"Nothing fancy, please."

"Just follow me."

. . .

WE TOOK ANOTHER PRIVATE ELEVATOR, rising to the roof. I was getting used to deluxe décor so I took the gilt and marble in stride, but the butler in dark jacket and striped trousers did impress me.

Michael said: "This is Albert. Used to work for the Queen at Buckingham Palace."

Albert nodded. "Sandringham actually, sir."

Michael looked puzzled.

"It's the Queen's country house," I said. It was all one to me, I had never had a butler.

"I'll call for you in the morning."

MICHAEL KALESTIAN GOT into a red Corvette, the clone of his car in California.

He guided the sleek vehicle through heavy traffic on the Strip, then headed east on Tropicana towards the residential suburb of Henderson.

Minutes later, he reached a long street of small homes with one-car garages. He slotted into a space by the kerb. He leaped out of the Corvette and bounded up a short flight of steps.

A curtain moved. He rang and the door swung open. A woman in a red silk robe embraced him. She looked a cut above her surroundings. Her auburn hair gleamed, as if freshly brushed. She smiled and pulled him inside.

After the door closed on that flurry, nothing

moved except a wisp of steam rising from the Corvette's scarlet hood.

AFTER MICHAEL LEFT, Albert and I eyed each other.

"May I show you round, sir?"

"Please do."

The suite was on two floors. I estimated 4,000 sq ft of space. The bathroom alone was half the size of my house in Santa Monica, with a marble tub and gold fittings.

"Can I fetch your bags, sir?" Albert looked about fifty with narrow eyes and a black goatee on a fleshy chin. His voice was low, as if deliberately pitched just below my own.

I confessed I had no bags, just the briefcase I had been clutching since Michael Kalestian whisked me into his 'plane.

"Albert, I just want to get some dinner and go to bed."

"Of course, sir."

I CALLED HOME. Magda asked, "How goes the hunt?"

"It's interesting, but I'm not learning much about Ara Kalestian. It seems nobody was close to the man."

"Perhaps he didn't allow it."

"Possibly. But I need something on his private life."

"Want me to snoop around? Maybe a library, or the Internet."

"You're a star."

"Call you tomorrow."

I hung up. I looked around for a telephone directory but, not finding one, went looking for Albert. He was next door, polishing silver.

"Is that silver real?"

"Yes, sir. All from Tiffany except for the steak knives, which were ground specially for us in Sheffield."

"Where can I get a good steak?"

"Our restaurant is outstanding."

"I feel like getting away from the hotel."

"You might try Palm."

"As in New York?"

"They have a branch at Caesar's."

Palm is a quirky New York eatery known for big steaks and rude waiters.

"That might work."

He picked up the phone.

I WALKED SOUTH on the teeming Strip, and stepped into the pseudo-Roman opulence of Caesar's Palace.

I sat down in Palm and ordered a rare sirloin and fried onions.

Albert's advice was spot on, the steak was perfect. The place was a definite improvement on Palm New York; the waiters were friendly and not given to rudeness. When I asked for the bill, I was waved off; it was taken care of. I was special. I was an Invited Guest.

Well, I could handle that.

Afterwards, I strolled back along the Strip.

To get into my suite, I had to wave my key card at a pad in the wall. The door opened silently. Because of this and the thick rugs, Albert was unaware of my arrival, so he continued to rummage through my briefcase.

It was empty except for a legal pad and some overdue bills. But the sight of Albert at his furtive work was a shock.

I did not confront him. I wanted to think. I turned and tiptoed out, leaving as quietly as I had entered.

I WENT DOWN to the casino and found a blackjack table with an empty seat. The dealer, a pretty Oriental in low-cut bodice and fishnet tights, smiled at me. A plastic badge on her chest said 'Tammy, San Francisco.' I sat down to play. The table minimum was ten dollars – about equal to my maximum.

I drew two aces. Statistics said I should split aces, so I put down another ten dollars and played them as two separate hands. It would buy me two good chances to win. Tammy dealt a seven to the first ace for eighteen and a nine to the other for twenty.

Tammy's smile was lovely but she had no conversation. She had a six showing. She turned up her hole card, a five and then drew a king. That gave her twenty-one, a winning hand. She scooped up my twenty dollars without a word. So much for statistics.

Mildly depressed, I went upstairs. This time I fumbled noisily and had a coughing fit, but it was unnecessary – Albert was gone. My briefcase lay where I had left it, looking untouched. The bed was turned down, a mint on the pillow.

I switched on the television and watched a program about Imelda Marcos, widow of the former president of the Philippines. It concerned $500 million that she and her husband were accused of stealing. The money was in Switzerland. The new Philippine government was trying to get the bank to release the money but there were rival claimants.

A judge had ordered the banks to release the money for the benefit of 9,000 victims of human rights abuse at the hands of the regime. But the banks were resisting. What if we paid the wrong claimants, they asked? Must they then give another $500 million to the right parties? Until the courts sorted things out, they were going to sit tight. So nobody was any richer, except the lawyers.

Marcos died in 1989. His wife was elected to congress by her adoring supporters, but she had gained weight and didn't look happy. There was film from the old days showing her slim and lovely, so there had been ups and downs for Imelda.

22

In London, the Honorable Quentin Teague strolled through Ludgate Square after visiting his tailor. He was thinking about Las Vegas and his meeting with Michael Kalestian.

Teague's love of risk-taking had fuelled a spectacular career. Six years ago he had borrowed money from his father and bought control of a tiny public company whose only asset was a defunct Malayan tin mine. He arranged for it to acquire a metal stamping business with a solid profit record. The stock soared. Now, many acquisitions later he was on paper one of the richest men in England.

Time for lunch. He bought a Financial Times and turned into Sweetings. He ordered his usual grilled sole and a glass of Sancerre and opened the paper. In Overseas News, he read a report he had been expecting:

"*CASINO WHIZ MURDERED*

Ara Kalestian, the Armenian fruit farmer who became the biggest landlord in Silicon Valley is dead at 56, shot by an unknown assailant in Los Angeles.

Kalestian was the largest shareholder in the 2,000-room Las Vegas Excelsior, the last major casino in private hands."

And more in that vein. Teague's brain raced as he reviewed his history with Kalestian.

They had met at the Excelsior shortly after Teague discovered Las Vegas.

He was already a keen gambler. His father had sneaked him into Crockfords as a teenager. Soon after, he discovered Monte Carlo, the queen of casinos. Years later, when one of his companies acquired a factory in El Monte, a drab suburb of Los Angeles, he got its manager to fly him to Las Vegas, just an hour away.

Many visits followed. He usually played at Caesar's but one day he visited the Excelsior on a whim. He fell behind playing blackjack but recovered and ended the evening $10,000 ahead. As he was leaving, a casino executive approached and asked if he had a minute to speak to the manager.

The manager was a slim man in a small office off the main floor.

"I'm Ara Kalestian."

"Teague."

They shook hands.

"Enjoying yourself?"

"Very much."

There was a companionable silence.

"Are you the owner?" Teague asked.

"For my sins."

"Ever think of selling?"

Kalestian laughed. "Are you buying?"

"I could arrange it."

"I know," said Kalestian. "I know quite a bit about you."

"Nothing good, I hope."

"You have strong nerves and a good attitude. We like that."

"I have credit at Caesar's."

"We would match that. How do you get here from England?"

"Via Los Angeles. It's an awkward journey."

"No private jet?"

"Private jets are extravagant."

"I agree. Next time, call us from L.A. and we'll send a plane for you."

From then on, Teague stayed at the Excelsior. He met Michael, who took care of his needs. Teague dated a few of Michael's working girls but without forming any regular attachment.

Then one evening there was a knock at the door of his suite. Grace Griffin, with a smile a mile wide, stood there as his dinner date, white teeth gleaming in contrast to her mahogany skin. They never did go out to dinner, establishing a pattern for the future.

He finished his meal and walked up Moorgate to his office. His lust for the dusky Grace was reason enough for another trip but also, prior to the shooting of Kalestian, he had scheduled a meeting with a certain attorney in Los Angeles. Its purpose was now doubly urgent.

He asked Pru, his not-quite-debutante secretary, to book a flight.

23

In seedy mid-town Las Vegas, Kathy got out of her car and straightened her short skirt.

She looked around. There were no casinos, just a few dusty motels, a Hispanic mini-mart behind iron bars, a bail bond office and a defunct gas station.

The sign over the computer store said 'Cheaptech – Best Prices."

Inside, the floor was stacked with computers in cardboard boxes. A couple of youngsters in UNLV sweatshirts were fingering the merchandise. She walked up to a display and pecked idly at a Dell notebook.

Blue-chinned Saddiq approached, in tan suit and white shirt, tie loose. He stood behind her, his hand over hers, guiding her fingers.

"It has a web-cam, so you can call your friends for free if you have Skype."

She smiled. "I'm just browsing, to be honest. I can't afford to get a new machine."

"The question is, can you afford not to? The new models have so many features." His confidence was infectious. The accent, the confiding smile and the smooth way he demonstrated the device. He had a salesman's gift.

He guessed she had a credit card, maybe for emergencies but it should have enough credit to cover the $399 price.

Just a small businessman in Las Vegas, plying his trade. Nothing to suggest that he was the paymaster for a fanatical, violent terrorist ring.

A chirp behind the counter told him he had incoming e-mail but he ignored it.

Suddenly, she smiled. "What the heck. I'll do it." She unzipped her Visa card.

"Fantastic. I'll get a fresh one from stock." He trotted off to fetch it. She took one of his cards from the stand on the counter.

He returned with the new machine in a colorful carton. As he was running her credit card, he asked, "Do you have a picture ID?"

She produced a Florida driver's licence. He saw she was 25, older than the usual student.

"Kathy eh? Charming name. New in town, Kathy?"

She smiled. "Yeah. Didn't get a Nevada license yet. Things are crazy with school starting."

"UNLV? What's your major?"

She flushed. "Divinity."

"Phone number?"

"Do you need that?"

"It's procedure. I have to follow the rules."

She gave him her number at the hotel. "I'll be getting an apartment, but that will work for now."

"No problem." He put the package in a big carrier bag with the name of the store and handed it to her with a flourish. "You're all set, Kathy."

His eyes followed her as she left the store. He watched through the plate glass as she crossed the sidewalk and got into her car. She waved at him before driving off. He turned back to the counter and read his messages.

There was one from the Camel. The man was a pest. He would reply later. He pulled up Kathy's record on the till roll and checked her phone number. He wrote it on a post-it note and slipped it into his wallet.

24

Harry Harley of Gametech was one of those annoying people who do breakfast well. He was 40, plump and smiling, always alert. Face pale, brown eyes close together. His hair was dishwater grey like his clothes – polyester sports jacket, grey pants, thick-soled Oxfords built to carry serious weight.

"Call me HH," he beamed. His grip was soft for a big man – although only medium height, he was broad, a solid two fifty. Short arms and a big belly gave him a penguin look, toes turned out. He laughed at every joke and also when he wasn't sure if it was a joke or not. Outside a Victorian-style music hall, I don't think I'd heard a laugh that came out 'Heh, heh', but that was Harley.

He ordered steak, eggs, half a melon and cereal. I ordered coffee.

"Good trip?" Michael Kalestian asked.

"The usual. Heh, heh."

"Are your masters happy?"

"Nope. Never are. Heh, heh."

He turned to me. "Executive committee meeting back east. Nobody there knows anything about gaming, so I'm the expert."

"What got them into casinos?"

"Lust for profit."

"So why are they not happy?"

"Profits not matched by cash flow. Cash is key for Gametech, it's their religion."

"Can you have profit without cash flow?" I asked.

"Easily, if you spend $50 million of it upgrading the casino."

Michael said wearily, "This is a long-running debate."

"Between?"

"Between the Kalestians on one hand, and our bankers and Gametech on the other."

"Bankers want cash? Who knew?"

"Of course. But business is tough. We must reinvest to keep up. Our guests demand more luxury, more services, more attention.

"How can you tempt more of them in?"

A silent pause.

"There's the Game," said Harley.

"What game?" I asked.

He looked as if he wished he hadn't spoken.

"Baccarat," said Michael quickly.

Harley nodded. "Yes, baccarat. We're making a feature of it."

He looked at his watch, stood up and stuck out a hand. "Duty calls. Great pleasure. Heh, heh!"

He couldn't retreat fast enough. He even left half his steak.

Maybe the game Carlton told me about in confidence wasn't as secret as he thought.

25

The phone rang in my suite. It was Kathy.

"You're in Las Vegas?" she asked.

"Yes."

"So am I."

Not good. Kathy's presence tends to complicate life.

"What are you up to?" I asked.

"I saw Carlton."

"And?"

"He has this creepy butler."

"Albert?"

"You know Albert?

"He's my butler too," I said.

"Where are you staying?"

"The Excelsior."

"In a suite?"

"I think that's what they're called."

"Damn."

I don't often render Kathy speechless. It's gratifying when I do.

"I caught him going through my briefcase," I said.

"Did you confront him?"

"He didn't see me."

She went on, "He eavesdropped on my conversation with Carlton, too. So I followed him when he went off duty. He went to a computer store."

"Is that bad?"

"No, but get this. I met the owner – name of Saddiq – and he's an even bigger creep."

"Good to know."

"Don't mock. They're up to something."

"You think?"

"I do. Carlton and his rich pals are up to something, too. He's being coy about it which is odd, he's normally delighted to show how smart he is. These other lowlifes want a piece of it, whatever it is. It's all connected."

"How can we find out more?" I asked. The way to get Kathy out of one's hair is to find her a project – as difficult as possible.

"They're spying on us. Pity we can't spy back," she mused

"Bug them somehow?"

"Now there's a thought."

26

Kathy found Saddiq's card. She screwed up her courage and telephoned him.

"You won't remember, but I bought a Dell laptop from you."

"Name?" sounding busy.

"Kathy Smith."

Normally, once Saddiq made a sale his interest in the customer ceased. He was not a hand-holder. If there was a problem, he referred the customer to the manufacturer's warranty. But sometimes a little hand-holding appealed. He pictured the pretty divinity student.

"Kathy, of course I remember. How are you, dear?"

She winced but forged ahead.

"There's a problem. It won't recognize my e-mail program."

"Probably just a setting. We can sort it out. Where are you staying?"

"The Bellagio."

Not cheap, far from it. He would have put her, as a college freshman, at the Motel 6 end of the scale. Perhaps her parents had money. Single girls were interesting, rich single girls doubly so.

He looked at his watch. "I'm closing soon, I could swing by your hotel."

Not what she had in mind. Her plan entailed some intimacy, but meeting in her hotel room posed risks. Letting the pushy salesman into her bedroom could cause all kinds of trouble.

"Okay but I'm in my car, and I'm near your store. Why don't I stop in?"

WHEN SHE GOT to the store it was empty, except for one customer on the point of leaving. When he left. Saddiq switched the door sign from 'Open' to 'Closed,' and smiled.

"Now we can focus on the problem."

She opened the computer lid. "See, when I switch on, it goes to the desktop, which is good. But when I click on the e-mail icon, I get 'Your program is not configured.' It's driving me nuts."

"Let's have a look." He moved nearer and tapped a key.

"I thought so. See, you have to say which programme you're using."

Their bodies were close now.

"Do I need to change it?"

He put an arm round her shoulder. "Only the first time. With the other hand, he pointed to an area on the screen. "Just type here."

She did so and a welcoming message filled the screen.

"You're so smart. I was so worried, after spending all that money. Thank you!"

This time, when his arm tightened round her shoulder, she responded by slipping her own arm round his waist and squeezing gently.

"What else can you show me?" she said.

"Do you want to set a default home page?"

She giggled. "I don't know what that means."

"Watch."

It did not take many more keystrokes before they were face to face and he was kissing her neck. She forced herself not to resist. Her hand slipped inside the waistband of his trousers and massaged his back.

The computer screen dimmed to save power but neither of them noticed. When his hand strayed lower and began to stroke her behind she disengaged.

"You're bad."

"There's an apartment upstairs."

'I'd love to, but I have a lecture. Orientation, it's compulsory."

"When can I see you?"

She was assembling her belongings.

"Call me tomorrow." Suppressing a shudder, she gave him a final kiss and swept out of the door.

As she drove off, he stood and watched, unaware of the weightless disk now attached by a tiny Velcro patch to the back of his shorts.

27

Carlton Tisch walked out of the Excelsior carrying a suitcase, to be met by leathery Kon Feaver and ushered into a black Jaguar.

Tisch got in. "You look tired," he said to Feaver who, in faded denim, looked as if he had been picking apples on a kibbutz,

"Getting here from the Keys is a hike."

Kon drove the sleek car onto the freeway and out towards the airport.

"Nice ride." Carlton fingered the soft leather.

"Thought you'd like it." Kon knew that Tisch, after an impoverished childhood, had a yen for life's finer things.

"Is Oliver finding anything?" he asked.

"He's trying. He's talking to the Kalestians, covering the bases, learning what he can."

"Should I speak to him?"

"Yes, find out what he knows. I didn't invest $2 million to have it go down the drain."

"What about Michael Kalestian?"

"He's a puzzle. His father swore up and down that the Game was secret, but now I find Michael knows all about it. His father left a letter to be opened in the event of his death, with full details, but the letter has gone missing."

"Was he afraid something would happen to him?"

"Possibly."

"Who else is in town?"

"Just me. Louise Chang went to L.A. She has an office in Chinatown. Teague flew back to London – something about a takeover. And our ponderous friend Baxter is on his yacht in Monte Carlo, so the group has dispersed." He stared out of the window. "I wonder what they're all up to."

"How did you get involved with this gang?" asked Kon. "It doesn't sound your speed."

Privately, Carlton agreed. Neon lights flashed by as he spoke.

"I seldom gamble, I think it's dumb. But some very bright people do. A year ago, I got a call from Teague, the roly-poly Brit. He doesn't look smart but he has a keen eye for a deal. I've made money with him. 'Got something you might like,' he said.

"He knows that what I really enjoy is making money. Not owning it, making it. He was willing to cross the Atlantic to talk and a few days later he turned up on Tortola in khakis, looking fit, quite different from the city-suited gent I was used to. We sat on my terrace and he explained.

'There's this guy Ara Kalestian.'

'I know the name', I said. 'Owns the Excelsior in Las Vegas.'

'Right. Anyway, he's onto something big.'

'Good for him.'

'What do you know about ex-dictators?' he asked.

'Most of them come to a sticky end. Look at Mobutu of Zaire, or Qaddafi in Libya. But what's interesting is how little of their money is ever found. Take Mobutu. Out of a rumoured $5 billion stolen, only $4 million has ever been recovered: one tenth of one per cent. Qaddafi: similar.'

'So?'

'I and some of Kalestian's other customers were on at him to find us a game with a high payout and he floated this idea.'

'What exactly?'

'He's made a study of the subject and he thinks he can lay hands on $400 million of that stolen money. He offered to put it up for grabs among the four of us,' said Teague.

'$100 million each?'

'No, winner take all. We would each start with $100 million and play poker with it until three of us are broke. The fourth player takes the whole pot.'

'Who are the players?'

'Me, two others and you, if you are in.'

'Who are the others?'

'I'll tell you if you come in.'

My instinct was to refuse, but Teague persisted.

'Don't think of it as gambling, more as funding an exploration,' he said. 'Mining companies do it all the time.'

'What's the ante?' I asked.

'$2 million.'

'That's a lot.'

'I paid it, and you're richer than me'

We both laughed. Neither of us keep score daily.

'I'll think about it.' I said.

'Don't take too long. I've got others interested.'

'Understood.'

"Here's the kicker, by the way,' Teague said. 'If Kalestian can't find the jackpot, he'll refund the ante.'

I thought about it.

"So there's only a one-in-four shot at the prize?"

'But the prize is $400 million. You all have an equal chance of winning. Better, if you play well.'

The idea was far-fetched, but I admit I was curious.

'What will the ante be used for?' I asked

Teague grinned. 'Bribes.'

That made sense. Ara would have to compensate whoever knew the whereabouts of the money.

As we were talking, my wife Mimi came out on the terrace. She had been painting and was wearing a paint-spattered tee shirt and cut-off jeans. She's English, like Teague. They met last year when we went to the races in England, and they got on well. They exchanged smiles now and I noticed him looking her up and down, but that's okay.

'What are you cooking up?' she asked.

'I'm trying to interest Carlton in a little flutter,' Teague laughed.

'Good,' she said. 'He could use some frivolity. All that Wall Street stuff is giving him grey hairs.'

So, out of a senile wish to please Mimi, I signed up. Once committed, I figured I should approach it like any other venture: get a jump on the competition by researching the heck out of the subject.

First I had to meet Kalestian.

I flew to Las Vegas. They gave me a suite at the Excelsior. There was a knock at the door and there was Kalestian. He is, or was, a dapper, smooth skinned Armenian-American, clean-shaven, five foot ten, courteous manner. He came in and we talked.

'Tell me this,' I said. 'If I give you $2 million, how can you guarantee that you will produce this big prize you speak of?'

He just smiled. 'I will.'

He had a good poker face, but I was sure he was hiding something.

'If I don't, I'll give you back your deposit,' he said.

'Can I have that in writing?'

'Sure. Write "Refundable deposit" in the corner of the check.'

So I did. It was pretty loose legally but at least he made the gesture.

'Who will you pay this money to?' I asked.

'That's my business.'

I gave him the check. I said, 'I want you to know I don't believe a word of all this.'

'No problem,' he said, smiling."

The Jaguar approached the airport. Kon stopped the car on the departure level.

"So that's the story," said Carlton. "Now he's dead and my money-back guarantee is useless."

"What will you do?" asked Kon.

"Go sailing." Carlton waved and strolled into the terminal.

.   .   .

BEFORE VISITING SADDIQ, Kathy had spent some time thinking about where to plant the bug. She wanted to ensure the device was live next time he said something interesting. Should she plant it in his office or his home? Finally she decided she should attach it to his clothing. But on which garment?

She noticed that he dressed expensively. His suits were from the pricier end of Armani and Calvin Klein. She assumed that he owned a number of them and varied his choice from day to day, so a bug in the waistband of his trousers was probably not the best idea.

His shirt was expensive, rich creamy cotton, but she noticed it was not clean that day, a small coffee stain on one cuff gave the game away. That set her thinking. A man in an Armani suit did not necessarily wear fresh underwear daily. Maybe once a week was good enough for Saddiq. So she gambled on the underpants strategy. It was a long shot anyway so what the heck?

After leaving the computer store, elated by the success of her plan so far, she hurried back to the hotel to install the other part of the plan – the receiver.

It was a rectangular box the size of a paperback book, solid-state with no motor to spoil reception. It was voice activated, starting up only when a signal came in.

She did not want to miss a moment, so she broke a golden rule and ordered supper from room service. As she was munching a forgettable $20 club sandwich, the device came to life and she heard a conversation that made the whole exercise worthwhile.

28

After what Kathy told me I wanted to talk to Carlton. I called his suite only to learn that he had left town. Not entirely surprised, I tried him on Tortola and finally got him face-to-face on Skype.

"You ran out on me."

"I had business here."

"New sails for your yacht?"

"Of course not. What do you want?"

What sort of game are you playing?"

"Are you trying to be rude?"

"I mean literally. You have some high stakes game going with your rich friends."

He said nothing.

"Who are the players?"

Grudgingly: "Sidney Baxter, Quentin Teague and Louise Chang."

"Baxter the publisher?"

"Yes. A piece of garbage."

"How so?"

"He gives a lot of money to charity but he has the worst business ethics ever, and I've seen a few tricks played."

And used a few, I thought.

"He's totally arrogant – and totally convinced of his own rightness."

Sounds familiar, I thought. "Why do you think he might have killed Kalestian?"

Carlton's phone slipped a few inches. He corrected it quickly but I caught a glimpse of Goneril up on blocks.

"He's chronically short of money."

"But he's a billionaire. It says so in the newspapers."

"Ah."

"What do you mean, 'ah?'"

"I'll leave it at that."

I changed the subject. "I know who Teague is, but what about Louise Chang?"

"Now there's a tough cookie. She can charm a tiger out of its stripes but underneath she's as hard as nails."

"From her name, I assume she's American born."

"No, she's from Hong Kong. Her given name was Liu which is Cantonese for willow and it's appropriate – the tree that bends but does not break."

"What's the chance she's our killer?"

"It's possible. There are stories."

"Stories?"

"Her husband was in real estate in Hong Kong. He secured an option to buy an attractive site for a high-rise office building. The underbidder was connected with Sun Yee On, one of the criminal Triads. They suggested to Chang that he sell them his option. When he refused, he was beaten up."

"Did he sell the option?"

"No. While he was recovering, Louise had power of attorney. She went to see the leaders of Wo Shing Wo, a rival triad and offered them a stake in exchange for protection."

"How did it turn out?"

"She built on the land. Then she sold out to Wo Shing Wo, retired from real estate and turned to shipping."

"Did she get full value from Wo Shing Wo?"

"No, she had to give them a huge discount. But she still walked away with millions. She also walked away from the Triad connection."

"Smart move."

"Said she was smart."

"None of that makes her a candidate for killing Kalestian."

"I forgot to mention one thing. That underbidder ..."

"Yes?"

"He turned up in a back alley in Kowloon, decapitated."

"That could have been the Triad, not Louise."

"Of course. But ..."

29

Kathy was excited when she called me that evening.

"You must hear this."

"Hear what?"

"I planted a bug on Saddiq."

"Saddiq?"

"The computer dealer."

"Slow down. Where did you get a bug? How did you plant it on this guy?"

"Never mind. You need to come over."

I strolled the quarter of a mile from the Excelsior to the Bellagio. It was a Vegas night, warm and black as velvet.

Kathy wore torn jeans and a blue tee-shirt with red and white letters saying "CSI Las Vegas." She saw me looking at it. "Eight bucks in Walgreens. The cheapest tee-shirt for sale in this hotel is thirty dollars."

"So what's happening?"

"Listen."

She pressed a button on a slim metal gadget. First, unidentifiable clicks and bumps. "Voice activated," she explained. "Wakes up when something happens. He's receiving a phone call."

"Hello?" The voice was gruff, with an accent I could not place.

"That's Saddiq," she said.

"Good morning." The second voice was flat, possibly Oriental.

"This was recorded at 7pm this evening," said Kathy. "If it's morning where the caller is, he would be about ten hours west of here. That puts him across the Pacific."

"What have you got for me?" It was the caller.

"I have a line on some major money."

"You said that before."

"My source is an actual signatory on the bank account. You can't get hotter than that."

"When?"

"Not long. I just need to set it up."

"I can't wait much longer. I've made plans."

"Care to share them?"

"No, it would compromise you. Need to know, as

you Americans say." The tone was ironic. Saddiq did not sound like an American, although he might be a recent immigrant.

"Who is your source?" It was the caller again.

"Also need to know," Saddiq fired back. "But he'll play ball. I have something on him, he won't dare not to."

"My operation is all set to go," said the caller. "I can't change the timing."

"Not a problem."

"It had better not be. Otherwise I may have to question your past accounting. There are rumours."

"Don't take that attitude with me," said Saddiq.

"I'm just saying. By the way, what about the person you said was competing with you?"

"Say again?"

"The young Englishman."

"Don't worry," said Saddiq, "I'll take care of that."

"How?"

"He will be dealt with."

There was more discussion, then the call ended.

"Good stuff, eh?" said Kathy.

"I have no idea what game they're playing."

"They?"

"Saddiq and his caller, Tisch and his gambling pals, Kalestian, the whole damn lot!"

"They are chasing some huge pot of money," she said.

"That much is clear."

"*They* includes you, by the way."

"Me?"

"I assume you are the young man they referred to. The one Saddiq said he would deal with."

30

Raoul Cerdan, a Filipino with signatory power over an account worth $400 million, checked the gold Rolex on his chubby wrist. He still had another two hours on Cathay Pacific's Boeing to Los Angeles, and an hour from L.A. to Las Vegas after that.

Frowning, he rearranged his bulky frame. It had been a long, tiring flight from Manila. Flying business class was a necessity when you were broad beamed like him, but even with the extra space it was a tight fit.

He was travelling unwillingly. He did not know what to expect in Las Vegas.

The phone call had come in the middle of the night. The caller was anonymous.

"Raoul?"

"Yes?"

He was in bed, but not with his wife. She had taken the children to their beach house. His maid, a dark-eyed beauty of sixteen, lay curled up beside him in the marital bed.

"Ara Kalestian is dead."

He had to think hard to remember who that was. Then, memory came flooding back. Confusion was followed by relief. If Kalestian was dead, was the monkey off his back? Had his shameful secret died also?

But relief gave way to fear. The caller apparently knew about his past.

"Who is this?"

"Never mind."

"I don't know anyone called Kalestian."

"Yes you do."

He tried to analyze the voice. The English was fluent but accented. It could be American. For sure it was not Filipino, which eliminated 80 million people. Nor did it sound like one of the rich egotists he regularly gambled with, or whose wives he had seduced. It was rough and with a note of menace as if its owner knew he controlled the situation, and controlled Raoul.

He tried remaining silent but the voice continued.

"We know about you."

"Don't you dare threaten me," said Raoul but his confidence was ebbing.

"You will be hearing from us."

The caller rang off.

That was a week ago.

Yesterday the second call came, summoning him to Las Vegas.

So here he was, with little more than his passport and some banking information that he had committed to memory. It would be his first visit to Las Vegas in five years. Last time, he had been slim and handsome, lusted after by the wives of his father's friends at the Manila country club where he played tennis at near-professional level. But now unused muscle was starting to turn to fat. His sensitive profile had gained an incipient double chin and the cupid's bow mouth resembled a fat Buddha.

Gambling and idleness had defined his life. His father was a successful attorney and friend of the ruling family. Raoul struggled through legal training and joined the family firm but his indolence soon made his father realize he could not trust him with serious projects, so he was given a public relations rôle. He led the life of a young clubman, making contacts and even getting to know the President.

One fine day he became a signatory on one of the Marcos bank accounts. The President himself suggested it as an emergency backup if the father was unavailable.

A year later his father had a major heart attack and retired but nobody remembered to change the trust agreement, so the confidence enjoyed by the father passed by default to his son.

Raoul discovered Las Vegas when he was still a student and made many trips to the desert city. He spent hours at the blackjack tables, a drink at his elbow. In a suite at the Excelsior he enjoyed a wide range of female company.

He came to the attention of Ara Kalestian, who supervised high-stakes activity. He accepted the Armenian's offer of credit. He continued to bet, and lost heavily. Kalestian grew concerned. After extending the young man's limit several times, he hinted that he might have to inform his father.

This was the last thing Raoul wanted. At home he had cultivated a reputation as a master gambler who always won. The loss of face would be humiliating. When Kalestian continued to press, to stave him off, Raoul emphasised his connection to the ruling family. He revealed that he was a signatory on some Marcos accounts.

To Ara Kalestian that was a thunderbolt. Here was a rare opportunity. The idea of the Game was born at that moment. Later, he refined the idea and it was polished and proposed to some of his wealthy customers. He promoted the Game as being based on a random hunt for hidden money, but Raoul was his secret ace in the hole. He might find other sources but if not, there was the young Filipino, safely under Kalestian's control.

The cabin lights came on. The aircraft was approaching Los Angeles, where Raoul would change planes for the last leg of his journey. He tightened his seat belt, resolving to plan for the best, but expect the worst. He landed in Las Vegas as dusk was falling and walked towards the exit. His summoner met him outside.

31

Next day, Saddiq was at the airport again, dropping Cerdan off for his return flight to Los Angeles. Things had gone well. His discussions with Cerdan, a mixture of carrot and stick, had resulted in a deal. Saddiq would gain major funds, in complete secrecy. So, as a reward, would Cerdan.

Neither of them trusted the other an inch. They would not beome friends, in fact they despised each other. Saddiq judged Cerdan to be weak and spoiled while the Filipino saw Saddiq as a common blackmailer.

But they knew they could help each other and they had worked out a way to make that happen.

But Saddiq still had one concern, a loose end: Oliver Steele. As long as Steele was following the trail, delving for information about Kalestian's death, there was a risk he would run across Raoul Cerdan. If that happened, Saddiq would lose all advantage. Cerdan would be strengthened because he could pit Steele and Saddiq against one another but Saddiq would end up with half a loaf or, Allah forbid, nothing.

Which reinforced Saddiq's intention. He must remove Steele from the equation. And, if things were not to spiral out of control, he must do so soon.

32

I breakfasted downstairs at the Excelsior buffet. When I got back to the suite, the message light was flashing. I was about to dial in when the phone rang.

"Hi," I said.

A man's voice asked, "Who is this?"

"Oliver Steele. Who wants to know?"

"Detective Pedro Gray, LAPD."

I remembered the voice and pictured the humorless face.

"Hi there, Detective."

"May I ask where you are, Mr Steele?"

"In Las Vegas, at the Excelsior Hotel. How's LA's finest?"

"I have bad news."

"Speak."

"It's about your house. It was broken into."

I didn't react strongly. Some people feel violated if their house is burgled, but what's a house? Just bricks and mortar, framing and drywall. I must either be well-adjusted or just plain insensitive. It's Carlton's house, not mine of course. I guess that cushioned the blow.

"Any damage?"

"There was a bomb. Half the building is destroyed."

This was ridiculous. "When did it happen?"

"About an hour ago. Neighbors heard the blast. The fire station is close to your house, so firefighters were there in minutes. They saved the place from complete destruction."

I took little comfort from that. It sounded like a huge loss.

"How did you find me?"

"Fortunately, your telephone was unharmed. I just pressed the redial button." He sounded pleased rather than sympathetic.

A thought struck me. "Is Magda there?"

"Excuse me?"

"My lodger Magda."

"There is nobody here except the firefighters."

I felt a chill at the back of my neck. "Is her car in the driveway?"

"Would that be a red Mazda sports car?"

"Yes, it would."

"It is here. The fire missed it. But . . ." Gray paused.

"What?"

"There's blood on the upholstery. Also blonde hairs and signs of a struggle."

It was the worst possible news. "You must find Magda. I'll be back today. I'll call you."

I hung up.

The message light was still winking. Gray said he had redialled the last number. The penny dropped. I dialed the message center.

Magda had called. I listened to her rich contralto.

"Are you there? I guess not. Hateful machine. But it says I can speak as long as I like, so here goes:

I have a lead on Kalestian. The internet was useless so I phoned a friend who works for the Global Enquirer and she had a look in their files. They store gossip the way the New York Times stores obituaries. They have a search algorithm: When two names occur in close proximity it rings a bell."

She went on: "Kalestian was the sort of low-key guy that doesn't give gossip columnists much scope. He was cautious, donating to both political parties. But a name did come up – Ann O'Shea. She's described as a dancer, which in Las Vegas can mean anything.

"She was the featured performer at a charity dinner he attended ten years ago – one of those glitzy events they're always having with Streisland or such. There are photos. She's good looking, I must say.

"Four years later they are sitting together at another dinner. Then six months ago, their names turn up again. This time Ann is on the committee of a rehab clinic – a Betty Ford type place – in Henderson. Kalestian is a donor, big time – a hundred grand.

"So there it is, your lead. When are you coming home? There's goulash, it's in the fridge."

The message was timed at 8am. It was now 10 o'clock. She must have called just before the explosion.

I set the receiver down.

"Albert!"

"Sir?"

"I need a rental car and a phone book."

"Yes, sir."

"Now!"

I set out for Henderson in a rented Chevy. I was shaken by the news from L.A. and wanted to get home but there was a call I must make first.

The Las Vegas area has been called a second Los Angeles and not in a nice way. In Henderson, spec builders have spawned rows of lookalike shoeboxes. 1121 Madison Close was the address listed in the phone book for Ann O'Shea. The street was a cul-de-sac, notable mainly for its lack of notable features. When I got there, it was 11am and already scorching. Hot air hit me like a club as I got out of my car. I rang the bell.

"Ann O'Shea?"

"Yes?"

She looked about thirty, voluptuous with white

skin and auburn hair. A red silk housecoat accented her figure.

"I'm Oliver Steele. I'd like to talk to you about Ara Kalestian."

"Are you a journalist?"

"No."

"Detective?"

"Not exactly. But I'm investigating his murder."

"You sound British."

"Half."

Blue eyes scanned me, head to toe. A long pause.

"Better come in, it's hot."

She waved me to an imitation Bauhaus chair and sat opposite. The living room was furnished modern. The latest Vanity Fair rubbed shoulders on a coffee table with the big book of Alcoholics Anonymous. Through French windows, bright green grass bordered a tiny blue pool.

She crossed her legs and adjusted her robe. The air-conditioning hummed.

"How did you find me?" A faint Irish accent.

"Through the phone book."

"You know what I mean. How did you get my name?"

"Research. Look, I'm not here to make trouble." I explained about Murray Segal in hospital, and the blood in Magda's car. She listened in silence.

"Does Modesta Kalestian know you are here?" she asked.

"No."

"Does she know my name?"

"Not from me."

"I wouldn't want the news that Ara kept a mistress in Las Vegas to compound her suffering." Heavy irony.

"I wouldn't worry about that." I pictured the implacable Modesta. "How did you and Ara meet?"

"He picked me up in a bar, at a dinner where I was singing, ten years ago."

"I thought you were a dancer."

"Singer, dancer. I have an act. I keep busy."

"I assume you don't drink." I indicated the book.

"Not lately."

"How lately?"

"Five years sober."

"You met Ara ten years ago?"

She nodded. "We would be together whenever he was in town, which was most of the time. We tried to keep it private. He came here."

"So, you saw him a lot."

"He spent more time with me than with his wife."

"Do you know her?"

"No. What's she like?"

"Religious."

"That's what I heard." She paused. "She knew he was seeing someone. She just didn't know my name."

I stood up and walked over to the window. There was a small wooden alligator in the pool, housing a thermometer.

"Did you discuss business?"

She thought for a moment. "We discussed his work, but without naming names. And I would hear him talking on the 'phone."

Oliver waited.

"Mostly confidential."

"Look, I could use some help," I said.

"He was working on this game, something that would distinguish the Excelsior from other casinos. It had to be big enough to attract very high-end gamblers."

"His son Michael told me how competitive things are," I said.

She brightened. "Have you been talking to Michael?"

I nodded. "What do you think of him?"

"I like him. He loves his job. He's like a kid in a candy store. We'll see how he does now."

"Do you see much of him?"

She paused again, then shook her head.

"I met him last year at some event." She looked down and fiddled with an ornament on the glass table.

I had not meant to cross-examine her, I was mostly there to gain background. But I got a strong feeling that she was lying.

I moved on. "What did he say about this so-called Game?"

She laughed. "The sums were huge. I couldn't relate. It was for people who were as rich as he, or even richer."

"Was he ready to launch it, so to speak?"

"I think he was close."

"Close to announcing? A press conference?"

"Not like that. Widespread publicity was not what he wanted. This was something for the few."

"Because the Game is illegal?"

"No, because of the notoriety. He never worried about legal niceties."

"How so?"

"If he got sued, he knew how to throw high-powered lawyers at the problem. Lawsuits against Ara would get tied up for years. He liked to joke that nothing was illegal until the Supreme Court said so."

I thought of Imelda Marcos. After seven years of lawsuits, thousands of abused Filipinos had not received one penny of the Marcos millions.

"For an entertainer, you seem to have a good grasp of business."

"One picks it up."

"How did the Game work?"

"I don't know. But he believed he could deliver a huge payout for the winner without using the Casino's money."

I got up to leave. "Now, here's a really big one. Can I look at your last few months 'phone bills?"

She knew what I had in mind. "You want the names of everyone I've been talking to?"

"Not you, him. It could mean life or death."

Long pause. Finally, "On one condition. Promise never to tell anyone who I am or where I live."

"Okay."

"Not anyone."

I promised. She seemed to accept my bona fides because she let me take the bills away and copy them.

34

F rom her house, I drove straight to the airport. I couldn't get a direct flight to LAX but I was able to catch a Southwest Airlines flight to Burbank. I boarded the aircraft with seconds to spare.

I used the seat-back phone to call my foreman Clyde, and asked him to meet me at the house. Then I called Detective Pedro Gray, who said he would be at Van Nuys police station.

There was an L.A. Times on the next seat. The headline: "Regency Casino gets Major Face-Lift." A big conglomerate had bought the Regency a few months ago. Now they planned to double the hotel's 1,500 rooms to 3,000, to compete with the MGM Grand and the Bellagio. The bill would exceed $900 million. Steve Los's argument about needing more capital made sense, apparently.

At Burbank I rented another car and drove to Santa Monica.

Half the building was gone. The bomb had destroyed the living room and there was a gaping hole in the roof. Rubble everywhere. My filing cabinet had disintegrated, its contents burned. None of my records could be salvaged.

Clyde shook his head. "Awesome." Still in his twenties, everything was either cool or a bummer. Awesome could mean either one.

I was not too upset about the house. Most of the papers were replaceable. I was more concerned about Magda.

Clyde said, "A guy called Hyman was looking for you. Said he could help."

Hyman was my neighbor, a computer engineer, retired from Hughes Aircraft, bald and amiable. His hobby was building computers and his garage over-flowed with circuit boards. I guessed he was going to offer to retrieve the data from my blackened computer.

He answered his doorbell.

"Hi, Hyman."

He was jumping with excitement. "I saw a car," he said.

"What sort of car?"

I was listening now. The street operates a 'Neighborhood Watch' system. Every day, a volunteer walks the area and writes down the license numbers of any cars not sporting a resident sticker.

"Dark blue Mercedes E-420, tinted windows. Not many of those around.

I had a vision of a blue Mercedes drawing away from Murray Segal's office.

"Was it near my house?"

"Two blocks away."

"Have you told the police?"

"No. I was about to call them when you arrived. Here's the number."

I jotted it down.

"I'm going to see the police now," I said.

"Give them the number," he said, excited.

I would think about that.

35

I left Clyde inspecting the damage and drove over the hill to Van Nuys Police Station. Pedro Gray came out and led me back to his desk in a grey-painted open area. The room was divided into cubicles. Smudgy memos were tacked up with push-pins. The layout made Gray look a lot less imposing. It was cold and people were wearing sweaters.

"Chilly," I said.

"They're supposed to come and fix the AC."

"Are you getting anywhere?"

He shuffled folders on his desk, peering through his spectacles. I guessed they related to Kalestian and to the bombing of my house.

"What's your take on all this?" As if he resented having to ask.

"Beats me," I said.

"We're treating the incidents as related."

No kidding. I spotted Murray Segal's manila envelope in one of the folders.

"Anything useful in that envelope?"

Gray shrugged. "Kalestian's tax return. Some lists of dividends. And some notes that I can't make much sense of. Mostly names and numbers. We ran them by Mr. Segal but he had little to add. He suggested they might refer to partnerships – Kalestian owned a lot of real estate jointly, with friends and family members."

He opened the envelope and showed me some yellow sheets. One bore a pencil list of four names, each followed by a date and a nine-digit number. I pushed it back, feigning non-interest.

Gray took out a nail file and dug under a finger-nail. "The young lady, your lodger?"

"Yes?"

"Any closer relationship?"

"No."

"We asked around the neighborhood. It seems quiet."

"It is."

I was about to mention the Mercedes but something made me hesitate. We eyed each other in silence. Gray yawned and I realized he was exhausted.

"How many unsolved murders do you have on your books?" I asked.

"About eighty. And a bunch of missing persons. Sorry I can't be more help."

He stood up. So did I. He said, "We shall need a photograph of Magda to circulate as a missing person. We'll do what we can."

"Okay," I said. "I'll be talking to the Kalestians. If you want to make a copy of that list I'll see if they recognize the names."

He must have been really bushed because he just picked up the paper and walked down the hall to the copier where he made a copy and handed it to me. I shook his hand and left.

Outside, I raced to my car and got the heck out of there, in case he had second thoughts and wanted his list back.

36

I asked Hyman if he could hack into to the DMV computer in Sacramento. He had top security clearance when he worked for Hughes. He also had the soul of a pirate. Within an hour he called me back:

"The Mercedes is registered to a corporation, Omega Delta Inc."

That gave me a starting point. My next stop was the Santa Monica Public Library.

I presented myself at the reference desk. The librarian was a Chinese-American girl with rimless glasses and straight black hair. She gave me a friendly smile.

"Do you have a directory of small businesses?"

"Of course."

Libraries are good. They don't care why you want something, they just help you, no questions asked. I was given a massive volume that listed every business within a hundred miles. Omega Delta, the owner of the Mercedes, claimed to be in import-export. It had less than fifty employees and under $10 million in sales.

I had fielded my share of phone calls from publishers myself and told some creative white lies, so I took that with a grain of salt. But I now had an address – Mulholland Towers on Lindley Avenue in Tarzana.

Tarzana is in the San Fernando valley. Way back, Edgar Rice Burroughs, the author of Tarzan of the Apes, bought the land and christened it Tarzana Ranch, and in 1928 the city surrounding the ranch took the same name.

I called Clyde from the car. "I'm going up to the Valley to check out an address."

"Need any help?"

"Maybe. Follow me up there. I'll meet you on the corner of Lindley and Van Nuys."

As usual it was baking hot in the Valley. Lindley was a tree-lined street off Ventura Boulevard, a couple of miles west of Murray Segal's office.

Mulholland Towers, twelve stories high, looked expensive. It had underground parking, reached by a downward ramp to the right of the lobby and guarded by a white roll-up grille. Security was apparently an issue.

I parked fifty yards away and waited. Clyde's red Jeep arrived and drove past without acknowledging me. I watched it drive on for a hundred yards and then pull over. My cellphone buzzed.

"I'm here."

"I see you. Stay in the car. I don't have a plan, but give me a minute."

I watched cars come and go for a while. Each time a car arrived, the white barrier would roll up in a smooth, well-oiled motion and close just as smoothly once they were inside. Presumably each driver had a remote. I saw late-model Volvos, Jaguars and Lexus – their owners seemed an affluent bunch. What I did not see was a blue Mercedes E-420.

But finally the gate slid silently upwards and the gleaming nose of a Mercedes emerged. The tinted windscreen made it difficult to see the driver but there was no mistaking the plate. Clean this time. It had been on my street the day before.

Pressing my phone's redial button, I called Clyde. "Here he comes."

"I see him."

"Don't lose him."

Clyde pulled out and fell in behind the

Mercedes. Both vehicles disappeared in the direction of Ventura Boulevard. I allowed five minutes, then drove back onto Ventura myself. I continued another two miles before stopping at Sam's Fantastic Deli. I needed to think.

37

Sam's is a chain of almost-Jewish delis. It lacks the authenticity of Canters or Langers, more a Hollywood dream of what a deli should look like. But the liverwurst is good and the sandwiches generous. For a brain needing food, they are the ticket. I ordered corned beef on rye and slathered on the mustard. I put my mind in neutral and scanned the Valley edition of the Times as I bit into the crusty bread.

I was about to discard the newspaper when I spotted the famous three-pointed star in an ad for a Mercedes dealership on Ventura Boulevard. Inspiration. I dialled the number.

"I need a hubcap for a Mercedes E-420."

The computer was consulted and gave its blessing.

"I'll be right round."

Too excited to finish my sandwich. In no time I was the proud owner of a shiny Mercedes hubcap and also significantly indebted to the Visa card people.

I drove to a side street and got out of the car. I unwrapped the hubcap and rubbed it around on the road. I wanted it to look as if it had come loose at speed and rolled along in the mud. A little artfully applied dirt, some spit and the job was done.

Then I returned to Mulholland Towers and parked in the forecourt. I ran a comb through my hair and presented myself, with hubcap, at the desk.

The porter looked me up and down. "How can I help you – sir?"

That pause before the 'sir' – ouch. He was thirty, his face red, manner curt. One of those near-robots who are the best that they can be – usually minus any sense of humour. Business cards in a little holder, like a doctor's office.

I proffered the hubcap. "This may belong to one of your residents."

He eyed it. "That so?"

"I was driving down Lindley when a blue Mercedes swung out of your garage. A few yards along, it threw this off. I stopped to pick it up, but when I looked around the car was gone.

He eyed me for a long minute. He had pimples

on his neck. Had I wasted my dollars? Finally he looked at his computer screen and said, "Must be Mr. Zafi in Penthouse A."

"Okay."

"He's not in."

"I know that," I said. "I saw him go out."

He eyed the hubcap.

"So, did you want to speak to him?"

"No, I want to return his hubcap."

"You can give it to me," said Redneck and held out a hand. I passed it over.

"You want to leave your name?" He asked the question as discouragingly as possible.

"No. Just doing my civic duty." He frowned, having trouble reconciling this idea with his success-based outlook. I took a card and left him trying to puzzle it out.

In the car, I called Clyde. "What's happening?"

"Not much. Our man went to the bank. Then he went to the Beverly Hills Hotel. He's having lunch with a guy."

"Where are you?"

"In the hotel bar."

"It's not cool to use your cell phone in a bar."

"Give me a break! There are three phone calls going on within six feet of me. All dudes in smart suits."

"Who's he lunching with?"

"Some fellow. Grey hair, briefcase. Could be an attorney."

"How far along are they?"

"Main course."

"Good. Here's the thing. I want to get inside Mulholland Towers but there's a porter. Not friendly."

"You need a diversion?"

"Exactly. Take down this phone number, it's the front desk."

"I want you to call him. Call from somewhere quiet, not the bar. You're an engineer from Cal Edison, checking the power supply."

"I'll get him to check the circuit breakers." Clyde understood things like alternating current.

"It's a modern block, maybe built in the eighties. The panel could be in a closet somewhere."

"I'm on it."

"Wait a bit though, I need to get into position."

"The time now is 1.44 and 18 seconds."

Clyde seldom smiled so I never knew when he was joking. My own watch is a battered Seiko Diver that has survived repeated immersion in the Cayman Trench, but it doesn't do digital.

"Give me five minutes."

"Okay."

"If he starts to head this way, for Pete's sake call me."

"Okay."

38

I like to be prepared, so I keep a few tools in the trunk of the Mustang including shears, a bolt cutter and a stud-finder for locating the uprights in a plasterboard wall. I stuffed these into my briefcase and took up position behind a large oak tree across the road from Mulholland Towers. From there I could watch the front desk.

I watched the porter pick up the phone and speak, presumably to Clyde. Then he walked across the lobby and disappeared.

I dashed for the lobby and looked around quickly. The elevator door was open and welcoming. I entered and pressed the penthouse button. The door slid shut and I exhaled in relief.

I stepped out into a broad lobby with hessian wallpaper and floral carpet. There were two penthouses, A and B. I walked past the door of Penthouse A, my footsteps falling silently, down the hall and through a door marked 'Exit.' Here, less elegant, were the back doors to the penthouses, and a metal staircase leading to the roof.

The door to the roof was padlocked but my bolt cutter sliced through the hasp and I was out on the roof, alone under the sun. I had a spectacular view of the San Fernando Valley, although marred by a carpet of yellow smog that hung biliously overhead.

Through a skylight I could look down into Zafi's apartment. Large living room facing east across the valley. I could see brocade sofas, a desk and some expensive looking furniture.

My phone rang. It was Clyde.

"Your man is leaving the restaurant"

"Alone?"

"No, with the other guy."

"Follow them," I said.

"Okay. You having fun?"

"I'm on the roof."

"Trying to get in?"

"Yes."

"A wall would be easier."

"Why?"

"Roofs are tough. Thick layers, weather-proofing."

I kicked the flat surface with my heel. Hard as concrete.

"What about the skylight?"

"Difficult. Steel frames, toughened glass."

I looked. He was probably right.

Clyde said, "He's moving."

"Don't let him see you." I rang off and went back down the metal stairs.

I looked around nervously but the place was deserted. I chose an area of wall near Zafi's back door. It might look solid but as a novice builder I knew better.

I placed the 'Zircon' stud-finder flat against the wallpaper and slid the device from side to side until the red light glowed, showing where the wall was reinforced by wooden beams. So I knew where it was hollow with just thin board between me and the other side. I chose a stud-free space a foot from the lock. In sunny L.A. where construction codes are sometimes disrespected and a penny saved is a penny in the contractor's pocket, it shouldn't be hard to punch through.

I felt some guilt, but not much. Lives were at stake. Some creative carpentry was justified. Don't try this trick in more substantial buildings, though.

I drilled holes at all four corners of a six inch square of particle board, hoping the other neighbors were either deaf or absent. With the shears, I snipped along each side, then tapped and watched the square of board fall between inner and outer wall. Then I cut a similar hole through the inner layer of board. I could now see straight into the apartment.

Reaching in through the hole, I groped around until I found the latch and opened the door. I was in. The whole process took less than fifteen minutes.

As I WAS ENTERING the apartment, my phone rang.

Clyde said, "He's heading your way."

"Alone?"

"Yeah. He dropped the other guy off."

"How close is he?"

"He's on the 405, heading north through the Pass. I'm guessing he'll take the 101 westbound and head for home. You can expect a visitor in about fifteen minutes."

"Call again when you're sure."

I stormed through the apartment, throwing open doors. It was a big airy place, decor a tad too perfect, shouting 'professional decorator.'

Most of the rooms revealed nothing, but two doors were locked, no key in sight. I studied the nearest. It was hinged to open inwards. Taking a short run, I delivered a smart kick just below the handle. Brass and wood parted and it flew open.

Inside, Magda reclined on a mattress looking thoughtful. She was handcuffed to the metal bed frame, naked as the day she was born, On a bedside table were empty food cartons, chopsticks, debris. The room was warm.

Apprehension gave way to relief as she recognized me.

"You took your time."

"I've been busy."

I set to work with the bolt cutter, snipping through the single handcuff. I started to massage her wrist but she detached herself gently.

"I'm fine. Can we please go somewhere else?"

"Is it 'come as you are?'"

She grimaced. "This is his idea of discouraging me from trying to escape."

"Did he, er . . ?" I paused. She shook her head.

"Nope. A perfect gentleman." She stood up and moved tentatively from foot to foot. "I'm short of exercise, though. I haven't left this room except to go to the john." She looked me up and down. "How about lending me that shirt?"

I peeled it off and handed it to her. "Let's go."

As we made for the door, an oddly dressed pair, my phone rang again. I heard labored breathing.

"Boss?" Clyde sounded weak.

"Yes?"

"Are you still in the apartment?"

"Yes."

"Better get out. He's only five minutes away."

"What happened?"

"He must have seen me. He circled round and slugged me from behind."

"Are you OK?"

"I guess. But you need to leave, fast."

I tugged Magda out of the front door and towards the elevators.

We waited impatiently. The light indicated an elevator was on its way up. I nodded at Magda. "That shirt suits you."

"I like it too."

As the elevator door slid open, instinct made me pull Magda aside. A grey-suited figure stepped past us, then swiveled round. His right hand went inside his jacket and came out holding not a camera but a snub-nosed automatic.

The Lord must have endowed me with a good sense of self-preservation because I raised the heavy drill and brought it down hard on his temple. The thud was sickening but the blow served its purpose. Zafi collapsed and lay on the carpet breathing noisily, blood trickling from his forehead.

I looked at Magda.

"Now what?" she asked.

"Help me get him inside." We took a leg each and dragged him into the apartment.

About to leave, I paused.

"We don't want him following us."

"Tie him up," said Magda.

"Do I detect some payback?"

"You sure do."

"What can we use?"

"Before the handcuff, he tied my wrists with electrical cord."

"Where should I look?"

"Beats me. But hurry, he'll be waking up."

I threw open various closet doors and finally found several yards of white electrical cable, which I used to tie Zafi's wrists and ankles, arranging him on his own living room floor like a chicken ready for market. Somewhat out of breath, I sank into one of the apartment's comfortable chairs and grinned at Magda.

"Let's go," she said.

"Almost ready." I looked around. We were in what decorators like to call a 'great room' – combined living room, dining and so on. A leather-topped desk stood by the window, strewn with papers as if Zafi had been working there before he broke for lunch. Might as well have a look.

A yellow notepad bore lines in what looked like Arabic. I had no idea if it was important, it could have been his grocery list. I tore off the page and put it in my pocket. There was a bank statement showing a balance of several thousand dollars. Also a manila folder with a typed label on its front, "The Game." I thrust it at Magda. "Hold onto this!"

"We'll look pretty bizarre walking the streets," said Magda. I was bare-chested, she in my business shirt.

I felt in Zafi's trouser pocket and found his keys, on a Mercedes ring. "Let's leave Mulholland Towers in style."

Back in the elevator, I punched "Parking" and we descended to the underground garage. Zafi's Mercedes was easy to spot. We piled in, anonymous behind the tinted windows. As we mounted the exit ramp, the gate rose automatically to let us out. I turned right on Lindley and drove a few yards before stopping behind my Mustang.

We switched cars. Abandoning the Mercedes, I guided the Mustang back onto the freeway. My last act on leaving Tarzana was to toss Zafi's car keys out of the window. They sailed in a graceful arc and disappeared into vegetation beside the road.

Magda was reading the manila folder as we drove. I dialled Van Nuys Police Station and asked to speak to Pedro Gray.

"Gray." Voice dry as ever. I pictured his pale face and horn rims.

"Oliver Steele, Pedro."

"Mr. Steele, how are you?" He did not sound very interested.

"I'm fine."

"How can I help you?"

"I have a present for you."

"Really?"

"If you take a ride to Mulholland Towers in Tarzana you will find it in Penthouse A, gift-wrapped."

"I'm too busy for games, Mr. Steele."

"A pity, because your gift is the killer of Ara Kalestian."

"What did you say?"

"In a bit of a hurry. Catch you later, Detective."

"Wait!"

I rang off feeling pleased, if childish.

39

W e covered ten miles of freeway before I realised we had nowhere to go. My house was a wreck. Even if we could stay there, the water and electricity were turned off. It was Friday and I had little hope of prodding the utility companies into action before the weekend.

Magda had a bad habit, when reading, of expressing amusement or surprise without enlightening the listener. She did so now, whistling and saying "Wow" several times. I finally said, "Magda, I'm under some stress. Either tell me what's going on, or shut up."

Pleased to have annoyed me – the Serbian never far below the surface – she said, "If I kept quiet, you'd be sorry."

"So speak!"

"This file is in several sections. First, a rule book for some kind of gambling game. Then a section about depositing money in offshore banks.

"Give me a summary."

As she read, things began to make sense. The foreign banks tied in with overseas phone calls Kalestian had made from his love nest in Henderson. The references to a 'Game' echoed what Ann O'Shea had said and what Harry Harley had also let slip – a game for rich people, the sort who could afford an ante of two million dollars.

Magda was now reciting the merits of tax havens in Switzerland, Belize and Vanuatu, wherever that was. In summary, there was a lot of money in these places, stashed by some pretty shady characters. The objective was to get hold of it. How was not spelled out.

"How much are they talking about?"

"$400 million."

"That's a lot of clams."

"Yeah. Maybe it's a misprint." She went on, "The third section is a list of names and addresses."

"Recognise any?"

"There's four of them." She read them aloud.

<u>Dr. Louise Chang</u>: Jardine Terrace, Victoria Peak, Hong Kong.

<u>Sidney Baxter:</u> MY Guinevere, Monte Carlo

<u>Carlton Tisch</u>: Box 29, Tortola, British Virgin Islands.

<u>The Hon. Quentin Teague</u>: Royal Avenue, Chelsea, London."

"Quite an international crowd," I said.

"I never heard of them, except for Carlton Tisch."

"You would have if you moved in certain circles."

"What circles?"

"The rich and famous. Baxter owns newspapers. Teague is a banker. Louise Chang is in shipping. All seriously well-heeled."

"What kind of address is MY Guinevere?" she mused.

"MY stands for motor yacht. Monte Carlo must be its home port."

"So Baxter lives on a boat. I had an uncle who did that, on the Danube. He wasn't rich, he was a bum."

"There are boats and boats."

"Do you think these are the players in the game?"

"Yes. This narrows the hunt for Zafi's employer."

"How?"

"They all want to get their hands on a certain list. It was in an envelope Ara was carrying when Zafi killed him. Zafi was about to steal it when Murray Segal stumbled onto the scene. In the commotion, the list got left behind. The police have it, but they don't understand it. I have a copy.

"What's on it?"

"Names of bank accounts. It, and this, are the key to the offshore funds."

"And our well-heeled friends are after the money?"

"Exactly."

"Is that it? That's the Game?"

"Yes."

"So one of the four players hired Zafi to steal the list from Kalestian?"

"And to kill him."

"Why kill the guy?"

"Whoever hired Zafi is greedy. He or she wants to keep the information to themselves. With Kalestian dead they can locate the money at their leisure, withdraw it and be home free before their rivals know what's happening."

Magda digested this as we hummed along the freeway.

"And you've got the list?"

"Right."

"Does that mean someone will come after you?"

"Probably."

She brightened. "So whoever does will be the villain. He or she will be Zafi's employer and responsible for the murder. And we shall know who it is."

"And I shall be dead. It may not be that simple, though."

"Why not?"

"I may hear from all of them. They all want the money."

"You know what I don't understand?"

"What?"

"Why would they do this? What's the point? They already live like kings, and have plenty left over."

"It's what they do. They're gamblers."

She shook her head in disbelief.

"So what now? Do we wait to be killed, like Kalestian?"

"Of course not."

"What then?"

I thought about it as we drove through the Sepulveda Pass. I was still thinking as we passed Getty Center Drive. Finally I said:

"We go underground."

"Huh?"

"Change our address, drop out of sight. Make sure nobody finds us. Not until we're ready to be found."

She looked unconvinced. "I hope you know what you're doing."

"It's the safest way."

"If you say so."

.   .   .

I PULLED off the freeway in Culver City and parked outside Penneys in Fox Hills Mall. I counted my money: $200. I gave it all to Magda.

"Buy some clothes. Stick to the basics, you can always go back later."

"Why not give me your credit card, I can sign your name, have some fun?"

I shook my head. "From now on, no credit cards."

In twenty minutes she was back looking trim in pink polo shirt and designer jeans, carrying several carrier bags.

"Do I get any change?" I asked.

She just smiled.

40

We drove to the Santa Monica branch of Wells Fargo, where I keep my money, and I asked to see the manager, Jay Lawrence. Jay is a guy with a future. He's smart and easy to deal with.

"I need $50,000 in cash." I have an account via a nominee company, a device to get round my bankruptcy issues. It's a grey area legally, but one does what one must.

He opened his mouth, then shut it and checked the computer.

"You have $7,000 in your checking account and $60,000 in Certificates of Deposit. You can either borrow against the CDs and pay interest, or redeem some and forfeit the income they are earning."

"Which way is better?"

"Redemption. The interest you lose would have been taxable, whereas if you borrow and pay us interest, it is not deductible. Uncle Sam wins either way." He smiled without humour.

"Do it."

When they brought the money, I counted off $10,000 and gave it to Magda.

Lawrence rolled his eyes. We shook hands. "Thanks, Jay."

"Good luck."

BACK ON THE ROAD, I explained. "It's easy to trace someone through his credit cards. Every transaction leaves a trail, whether it's a restaurant, an airline or whatever. The guy we are avoiding would find us in a minute. From now on we pay cash."

"Even so, fifty grand?"

"Ever tried to live without credit cards? What about renting a car? How much deposit do you think they want? Besides, I rather enjoy walking out of a bank with fifty grand in used bills."

We headed west on Wilshire.

"Where are we going now?"

"Beverly Hills. Steele's first rule of invisibility is, 'Be anonymous but be comfortable.' Only losers hang out in second rate dives."

The Nikko Hotel, a Japanese-owned five-star

establishment, was one of Los Angeles' best kept secrets. From the moment you pull off noisy La Cienega, you enter a serene world, an oasis of good taste in a brash city. The hotel is impeccably managed by a German, Gunther Obermeyer. The atrium has an elaborate Japanese water garden with little streams running under stone bridges and fountains splashing into pools. Perfect flower arrangements delight the eye. One could be in rural Japan, not just north of L.A.'s tacky Restaurant Row.

At the desk – a long, gleaming slab of black granite – I asked for a suite. Herr Obermayer himself appeared.

"Mr. Steele, how delightful! Madame . . ." he kissed Magda's hand, coaxing a smile and finessing the question of our relationship.

I drew him aside and peeled off another ten thousand. "I want to pay for everything in cash. I don't want certain people to know where we are. Accept no calls. We were never here. We shall charge everything to the room and you can apply this deposit. Tell me when to top it up."

"Understood."

I indicated the remaining thirty grand. "Can you look after this?"

He signaled the receptionist. "A safe deposit box for Mr. Steele. And give him the Kyoto Suite." He bowed. "Enjoy!"

We had two bedrooms and a comfortable sitting room facing north. There were paper screens in place of curtains. Afternoon sun glinted on the white HOLLYWOOD sign in the distance.

Magda yawned. "I'm ready to crash." She pottered round, trying out the terry bathrobes and scented soap. Then hugged me and retired.

I telephoned the Kalestian estate and spoke to Modesta Kalestian.

"What progress, Mr Steele?"

I related my adventures with photographer Zafi and explained that there were still questions to be answered. But that Zafi was clearly working for one of the Game-playing foursome.

"I shall have expenses," I added. I was willing to explain, but she interrupted.

"I will cover everything."

"It may mean foreign travel."

"What's the most it could amount to?"

I hesitated. "$20,000."

"I'll mail a check."

"Not to me. Can you send it to my bank?"

"Of course."

My next call was to Clyde.

"How are you?"

"My skull is split in half."

"What happened?"

"I'm not really sure. I was following the Mercedes. We had turned off the freeway and were approaching Tarzana. The Merc ran a red light. I waited at the light. Next thing I know, I'm hit on the head. I guess he turned off and doubled back. I woke up with six cars honking and no Merc. I'll live, but how are you?"

"We're fine. And we left our friend Zafi neatly secured. Van Nuys police should have arrested him by now."

There was a pause.

"'Fraid not," said Clyde.

"What do you mean?"

"When I came to, I drove straight to Mulholland. The police were already there – squad cars, blue lights."

"I called them," I said. "I left Zafi tied up with electrical cable."

"Guess he pulled a Houdini on you. I saw police coming out carrying loose cable, but no suspect."

I cursed quietly. Just when I thought we had won a round. I felt especially foolish because I had told Modesta that Zafi was in custody.

At least Magda was safe and the two of us were still free and able to make trouble. But Zafi was free too, and probably out for blood.

"Do this," I told Clyde. "Start fixing my house up.

Make sure the phone and answering machine are in good shape. I want to be accessible. People are going to be calling and I want to speak to them, but not face to face."

"Anything else?"

"Come and have brunch tomorrow and we'll make a plan."

"Okay," said Clyde. "Just one question."

"Yes?"

"Where?"

I was about to name the hotel, but hesitated. What if someone was listening in?

Someone said, only the paranoid survive but, as someone else said, even paranoids have enemies. I had enemies.

"Remember where we had lunch last year with the Mayor of Culver City?"

"Do I?"

"Sure you do. You were bidding on the contract to rebuild the Fire Station."

"Oh. Yeah."

"Meet us there."

"Okay."

Me, the poor man's Howard Hughes.

WEEKEND BRUNCH at the Nikko is memorable. The setting is elegant and the buffet lavish, everything from caviar to smoked salmon – not the thin super-market stuff but the real thing, smoked in some Scottish crofter's chimney.

We sat under colored umbrellas, watching an army of chefs barbecue giant shrimp. Next to the grill were a four-foot poached salmon and a huge side of rare roast beef on a silver dish. A twelve-piece band played Glen Miller. A man in a ginger wig danced the foxtrot with a girl who was not his niece. A couple of actors in reflector shades tried to pretend they didn't care if nobody recognised them.

"Your phone is live," Clyde told me, "The answering machine is on."

"How do I pick up messages?"

"Here's your access code. When you hear the tone, key it in. Try it!"

Using my mobile, I dialed home and punched in the code.

There were some hang-ups and people selling insurance. Then a polite message got my attention.

"Mr Steele, please call the office of Dr. Louise Chang. She wishes to speak to you."

Louise Chang of Victoria Peak, Hong Kong.

The voice gave a Los Angeles number.

"This could get interesting." I dialed.

"Chang Shipping, may I help?"

"Dr Chang, please."

"Senior or Junior?"

I hesitated. "Dr Louise."

"One moment."

I heard the line being transfered.

"This is Terence Chang." Young, brusque.

"Dr Chang, please."

"This is her grandson. How can I help you?"

"This is Oliver Steele."

"Ah yes. She wishes to see you at four o'clock. Our office is in Chinatown. Do you need directions?"

"Whoa," I said. "What if I don't feel like coming down town?"

There was a pause.

"My grandmother is elderly. She does not travel very much."

"My mother is 80 and she flies all over the world."

"One moment."

A woman's voice, fainter but with more authority.

"Mr Steele, how are you?"

"I'm fine. How are you?"

"Very well." The voice had a precise, agreeable tone. "I understand you obtained some information from the late Ara Kalestian."

"I did?"

"I'd like to discuss it."

"You and others."

Another longish silence. Finally she said, "Do you think we would communicate better in person?"

A touch of humour? I found myself agreeing.

"I'll be happy to come and see you," she said. This Oriental was not concerned about saving face. I made a decision.

"That's not necessary. Give me your address."

41

Half an hour later I was in Chinatown.

Chinatown in Los Angeles is sun-bleached and flat, very different from its better-known counterpart up north. There are banks with exotic names and dozens of restaurants, from cramped seafood cafés to big pavilions serving dim sum to hundreds. Live turtles splash in tanks in supermarkets whose shelves are stocked with taste bud-curdling sweet pastries. It does not depend on tourists. Some of the real estate is more expensive than Beverly Hills.

Chang Shipping was sandwiched between a wholesale jeweler and Little Joe's Italian, popular with Dodgers from nearby Chavez Ravine.

The man in the outer office could be the grand-son. He waved me through and I met Louise Chang, a slim woman dressed in slacks and short-sleeved shirt. They say the Chinese do not show their age and that was certainly true of Louise. Her ivory skin was stretched smooth over flat cheekbones. Only faint liver spots on the hand she extended hinted at her age. I shook it carefully but her grip was firm.

"A pleasure." The hollow voice was warmer when offset by her smile.

"The pleasure's mine."

She nodded. "Do you have the account numbers?"

For a moment I was confused. Then I realised she meant Kalestian's list. She was wasting no time. I think she assumed that I knew more than I really did. I tried to look cool.

"I don't see how they can be any use to you," she said.

The difference between salesmen and accountants is that, when in doubt, a salesman does something – anything. An accountant does nothing. I did nothing.

She was looking at me oddly. Was I overdoing it?

"Yes and no," I said.

She smiled as if she guessed I was winging it. This was one of the world's most successful businesswomen. I might be a bit out of my league.

She waved a hand as if to say, let's be frank. "This is an unusual situation for you."

"That's fair to say."

"I'm sure you want to be done with the matter. I, on the other hand, have an interest in those bank accounts."

"A financial interest?"

"Of course. I've put a lot of money towards obtaining the information."

Did that give her any legal rights? Probably didn't matter either way.

Chang sighed. "Let's discuss compensation. You've been seriously inconvenienced. A week ago, your life was under control. Then you were hired to investigate a murder and now your own life is at risk."

"Things *have* gotten a bit hectic."

"I will buy the list. For a fair price. As soon as I do, others who want the list will leave you alone. You can resume your normal life."

"How dull." The words slipped out.

Her eyes narrowed. "Ah! This is exciting? Like the movies?"

I said nothing.

"You must be careful."

Was I being threatened or just patronized?

"There are forces you are not used to. Some tough cookies." The Americanism fell oddly from her lips.

"Tougher than some of the goons I come across in the building game?"

"Maybe not tougher, but more effective. They have the power to hurt you."

I said, "Why do you want the list so badly?"

"What if I said I wanted to return a great deal of money to its rightful owners?"

"Namely?"

"Those from whom it was stolen. In a country near my own."

I waited, but that was all she would say.

"I'd like to believe you," I said. "But to me the money looks like part of a game for bored billionaires. Of whom, with respect, you are one."

"I will give you a hundred thousand dollars in cash for the list."

"No. Even if I said yes, how do you know I would not make copies?"

She smiled. "I have resources. People honor their agreements with me."

A very polite threat. I said: "Your offer's much too low. The list is worth millions of dollars. But the matter is moot because it's not for sale."

"You may regret that." The smile had faded.

"Pehaps." I started towards the door. "Please excuse me, I have work to do."

"Work?"

"Finding out who ordered the killing of Ara Kalestian. I promised his widow."

She looked surprised. "Who exactly are you working for?" she asked.

"Good question," I said. I had started out working for Carlton Tisch. Then I found myself loosely aligned with Modesta Kalestian.

"I'm working for the good guys," I said brightly.

We shook hands.

She smiled. "Nice to meet you."

42

I retrieved my car from the park across the street. I had plenty to think about. Was Louise Chang on the side of the angels, as she claimed? She could just as easily be the one who had set Zafi on Ara Kalestian, and on me.

As I drove through Chinatown, I began to suspect that I was being followed. By the time I got on the freeway, I was sure of it. The car was a red Thunderbird, not an inconspicuous car – whoever it was, they were doing a clumsy job and I was able to keep them in my rear-view mirror. I could not see the driver because the afternoon sun reflected into my eyes, but I had my suspicions.

I did not want to be traced back to the hotel so I left the freeway at Bundy Drive and drove to a squash club where I sometimes play, Center Courts in Santa Monica, managed by shrewd businessman Gary Gullette and the lovely Patti Sogaard.

I parked alongside the building and, grabbing a racquet from the trunk, went inside. From one eye I saw the nose of the T-Bird inch into view.

The air rang with the din of rubber balls. Australian pro Grant Pinnington was coaching a teenager. Grant was one of the world's top players and has one of the hardest crash volleys in the game. I watched him decoy his opponent with a corkscrew lob. When the young man returned the ball, Grant buried it in the nick with a shot of thunderous power. He turned and grinned at the spectators.

"Okay to use the back exit?" I asked.

"No worries, mate."

I hurried through to the door that said "Fire Exit Only."

I jumped back in my car and got out of there. I glimpsed an angry Chang grandson, wrong-footed, sprinting towards his car, but I was well clear. Two quick turns and I rejoined the freeway minus the T-Bird. I returned to the hotel in good humour.

Magda was watching C-Span and looking bored.

"How was Mrs. Chang?" she asked.

"Inscrutable."

I checked my answering machine. One message, scratchy as if from afar.

The voice was rich and deep, forceful but ingratiating. The accent was educated English, but with a timbre that suggested central Europe. It belonged to someone I had heard of but not met so the friendliness rang false.

"Mr. Steele, this is Sidney Baxter calling from my yacht in Monte Carlo."

Like warm treacle being poured into my ear.

"We must meet, dear boy, we have so much to discuss. Come to dinner, my chef is the finest in Europe."

I handed the phone to Magda.

"Oily piece of work," she said.

"Where do you think he's from?"

She shrugged. "His English is perfect."

"Too perfect?"

"Maybe."

"Like Zoltan Karpathy? Could be Hungarian?" I asked.

"Or Czech. I'll look it up."

"That'd be great."

Next, I called accountant Murray Segal.

"Murray, it's Oliver Steele."

"What do you want?"

"You sound pleased to hear from me."

"I'm tired. I've spent all day at the IRS, defending a client on tax fraud. What do you want?"

"I need an expert on offshore bank accounts. Do you know one?"

He laughed. "The best experts are drug dealers."

"What about your entertainment clients? Don't some of them open offshore accounts to avoid taxes?"

"I steer clear of that stuff. Some attorneys promote offshore trusts which they swear blind are totally legal, but they mostly collapse when the IRS starts digging in."

He paused. "There is one attorney I've used, though: Victor Aronson. He wrote the book on the subject."

"Give me his number. I'll go see him on Monday."

"He's in London."

"When will he be back?"

"He lives there. He's English."

"Give me his number anyway."

Befor he left Las Vegas for Los Angeles, Oliver told Kathy to keep monitoring Saddiq, using the tiny electronic bug.

She did her best. Transmission continued for two days. Besides English, there were several conversations in Arabic which eluded her understanding completely.

The final transmission sounded like splashing, followed by bumps and thuds. She was mystified until she realised that it was the noise made by a washing machine filling with water and then beginning the wash cycle. Laundry day chez Saddiq had finally arrived. After a minute, transmission ceased. She assumed the bug suffered a tragic death by drowning.

She telephoned Oliver and broke the news. The

Arabic conversations were a total loss, but she was able to describe the discussions between Saddiq and the Filipino Raoul Cerdan, which had been conducted in English.

In a nutshell: Cerdan controlled more than $400 million in an offshore account. Under pressure, in exchange for a hefty bribe, he would reluctantly pay it to Saddiq. She could not tell which bank was involved, or where. But it confirmed for Oliver that, in continuing his search for the funds, he was on the right track.

44

Few of us are without vanity and I have my share – I like to keep my waistline under control. Once a week I go off to the South Bay Squash Club where I play with a few like-minded souls. None of us are fully fit. Our best player Greg Stiles has played so much squash that his knees are bone on bone, Alan Fox has issues with arthritis and Alec Anderson wears a stainless steel hinge on his knee. Only physician Sandy Clark is almost whole. We scramble around the court for an hour, shower and go our separate ways feeling virtuous and a tad fitter.

I must have looked preoccupied because Stanford-educated attorney Fox said, "You were rubbish. What's wrong?"

"Thought I was up to par."

"He's right, it was noticeable," said Anderson in his Scottish burr. He was one of many squash players in L.A. who are exiled Brits working for the aerospace companies.

"Can't always be on top form," I said. But it made me wonder if the pressure was getting to me.

I was the last to leave. I unlocked my car in the dark alley outside the courts. The club is in Torrance, in a not-great area a long way from the bright lights. It was created by the members themselves including Alec and physician Bob Bloomfield and was an unattended lock-up, so there was nobody around.

The first intimation of danger was a gun in the small of my back.

"Turn round."

Three of them, all armed. Two backed away but kept their weapons trained on my stomach. Resistance would have been foolish.

The third man was too well dressed to be a chance mugger. "Good evening, Mr. Steele."

"What's this?"

"I think you know."

"Saddiq?"

He smiled, which frightened me. "I don't understand," I said, "We're not in competition. I just want to find out who killed Kalestian."

He shook his head. "Not me."

"Then you've committed no crime. Why would my presence bother you?"

"Ara Kalestian had something I want. You might find it before me."

Money, obviously. I added two and two but they only made three. Try bluff:

"I have information that you need."

He raised his weapon, a silenced Walther, and aimed it at my heart.

"You won't meet Cerdan now, so my deal is safe."

Cerdan, that name again.

I could see his pale finger tightening on the trigger.

45

D rop your weapons and lie flat on the ground."

The words came from a megaphone, deafeningly loud and unexpected.

Blinding spotlights. Red laser dots on the torsos of Saddiq and his companions.

Saddiq made a quick assessment and tossed his gun on the ground. He fell to his expensively trousered knees. One colleague followed his example. The other melted away into the night.

Sharpshooters in flak jackets, people yelling, the works. Los Angeles police are not noted for their subtlety. The Arabs were pushed down and handcuffed.

So was I. The ties were painful. I suppose it's prudent to take no chances when you aren't sure who are the bad guys but I still didn't appreciate the treatment. It took half an hour of questioning by an individual in plain clothes who refused to identify himself before they stopped shouting, but finally the ties were cut and I could rub the circulation back into my insulted wrists.

I remained puzzled. Only later did I learn of the database search by Secretary Altman, prompted by Senator Ham, that led to Saddiq's arrest.

My confusion may have worked to my advantage. That and my membership card in the California Society of CPAs. We know that U.S. law forbids racial profiling so it couldn't have been my blue eyes and British accent.

Saddiq and his henchman were less lucky, having swarthy complexions and accents not from a British university. Saddiq did not help his case by firing bursts of Arabic at his companion, which earned him a hard shove and an invitation to shut his mouth. I assumed he was telling the man, "Keep quiet and let me do the talking."

Things finally quietened down. As I was getting into my car I heard Saddiq demanding a lawyer. The plainclothes guy said something about the Patriot Act, so I didn't give Saddiq much chance with that.

I wish I'd had a chance to ask him about Cerdan.

· · ·

Twenty minutes later I was back at the Nikko enjoying grilled lobster and a glass of Sancerre in the Pangaea Grill with Magda.

I tried to make sense of the evening.

"What should I do next?" I asked her. I have no false pride about Magda. She speaks slowly but thinks twice as fast as I do.

"That depends what you're trying to achieve."

"Same as ever. Find Ara's killer and Carlton's money."

"And stay alive?"

"That too."

"Saddiq didn't kill Kalestian," she said.

"I don't think so either, but what's your reasoning?"

"Because, when he denied it, he was about to shoot you. Why would he lie?"

"Good point. So we're down to Carlton Tisch's three gambling buddies – the last suspects."

"Four, if you include Michael Kalestian."

I nodded. "And five including Carlton. Don't forget him."

"Are you serious?"

"He's ruthless enough, and also devious enough to deny it."

She let that sink in. "Is Saddiq out of our hair?"

"For sure. If he's suspected of laundering money for Al Qaeda they'll lock him up and lose the key."

"I bet they'll sweat him. He must know some useful stuff," she said.

"The U.S. doesn't use torture."

She gave me a look. "How do you spell 'extraordinary rendition?'"

For a moment I almost felt sorry for Saddiq.

She dabbed her mouth with a pink Nikko napkin. "Let's review. We know certain bank accounts were of keen interest to Saddiq and to Ara, both of whom are now out of commission. The man Cerdan seems to be significant. What do we know about him?"

"Not much; at present it's just a name."

"I'll do some digging," she said.

NEXT MORNING AFTER COFFEE, she led me to a desktop computer in the hotel's business area.

"First, I googled Baxter. He checked out."

"Meaning?"

"He checked out. Get it?"

"No."

"Checked."

I finally understood. Baxter was Czech.

"Very witty."

She nodded, satisfied. "I also googled Cerdan. Marcel Cerdan was one of France's greatest boxers. Had a famous love affair with Edith Piaf."

"I actually knew that. Not our man, though."

"No, but then I struck gold. Cerdan and Company, a law firm in Manila. Experts in international tax. Here's their website."

There was a list of the firm's partners, six of them. The senior partner was Raoul Cerdan.

Head-and-shoulders of a smiling, solid-looking man in his sixties, everyone's idea of a trustworthy attorney. His speciality, estate planning. No alarm bells; didn't look as if he would touch high stakes gambling.

But lower down was another Raoul, his son. Wavy hair, big smile, playboy look. No specialty listed, probably didn't have one. Much more promising.

"He looks like the one."

I nodded. "I'm starting to think we're on the track. Not sure how, but my irrational confidence is building up."

"Enough for you to make that European trip?"

I looked at my watch. "Wonder if I can make a flight to London this afternoon."

"I might join you."

"Don't know if Carlton would spring for that."

"On my own dime. Haven't been to the British Museum in a while. You have another message, by the way."

"From?"

"Your boss Carlton."

"He's not my boss."

"What is he?"

"A client."

"Pretty big client."

I'm touchy about that. Truth is, Carlton accounts for most of my income. My bankruptcy complicates things. When I went broke I was underwater by a million pounds. I've paid off half of that, thanks to the Caribbean job, but I still have a long way to go. Carlton is my best chance of amassing enough clams to pay it in full, but I don't like being reminded of the fact.

"He's on Tortola and he wants to talk to you."

Tortola is Carlton's real home, his favourite. He also has a brownstone on the Upper East Side, an estate on Long Island and the Santa Monica house. He bought Santa Monica because he thought he should be invested in California real estate but after one trip he never went back. He says California people are too damn happy, presumably meaning they are not sour apples like him.

He built the house on Tortola from scratch. He was sailing past the island one day and thought it would be a neat place to build a home. Nice to be able to do that. It's expensively simple, a series of Island style cedar cabins with copper roofs, cascading down the side of the hill. Full-height windows open to let the breeze waft through.

The first time I was there I asked about hurricanes. He pulled out the plans and showed me how its piles were anchored deep in the rock and its walls could sway slightly to absorb gusts up to 200 miles an hour. He doesn't do things by halves.

I called him.

"What's going on?" he said, brusque as ever.

"Not much. I'm going to Europe."

"Why?"

I told him about Sidney Baxter's invitation.

He grunted. "What's this nonsense about al Qaeda?"

"How did you know about that?" Then I realized Kathy must have been keeping him informed. I just wish she had reported through me, rather than around me.

I explained that Saddiq had been arrested.

"And you were almost shot?"

"I escaped."

"Through no fault of your own."

"Meaning?"

"The FBI picked your chestnuts out of the fire."

"Some might see it that way."

"You had better come and see me."

"Must I?"

"There are some sensitive matters to discuss. Tortola is on the way to Europe, it's an easy detour."

Actually, it wasn't. Might look that way on the map but there are no direct flights to Tortola from any US city. This is no accident. Tortolans, who include some well-heeled folk with famous names, don't want a tourist influx. To get to Tortola you have to change in Puerto Rico which is never fun. I would need to change again for the onward flight to London, so it meant jumping on and off a series of planes, for the doubtful pleasure of a chat with Carlton.

But he was adamant, so the next day found me in a rented car, bumping uncomfortably along the rutted drive to his cliff-top retreat.

He was sitting on the terrace, overlooking the sparkling blue Sir Francis Drake Channel eighty feet below, in grimy khaki shorts and a Yankees cap, a small Star of David nestling in his grey chest hair.

A folder of papers and an open Budweiser on the table. I knew he wouldn't offer me one so I strolled into the kitchen and helped myself.

"Well, young man, what have you found out?"

"Not much."

"What am I paying you for then?"

"You haven't paid me anything yet."

"You need to take a closer look at Teague."

He meant the English banker, a member of his high-stakes game.

"If you say so."

"He's ruthless."

"Do you think he had Kalestian killed?"

"I wouldn't put it past him."

This negativity was surprising because I knew of Quentin Teague as a colleague of Carlton's, not an adversary. During the Casino Caribbean affair, the two men had planned to float an internet casino on the London Stock Exchange. London, because offshore gambling was illegal in the United States. British law was more permissive.

If the plan had worked, it would have been a marriage made in hell. Unfortunately for the two partners, the market for gambling shares collapsed at the crucial moment and the project was aborted, but that was not the fault of either man, so it was hard to see why they had fallen out.

"I thought he was a chum of yours," I said.

Carlton sniffed. "He's too clever by half."

When Carlton said something like that it usually meant he had been outwitted.

His eyes flickered towards a folder on the table and I picked it up. It was an offer document – the hundred pages of small print that define an offer by one company to invest in another.

In this case the investor was Transient Holdings,

a Bermuda-based subsidiary of Carlton's master company. The target was a company called Keystone Guarantee.

The offer was summed up on the front page:

"Issue of £80,000,000 in 12% Cumulative Convertible Participating Preference Shares."

"Catchy title." I said.

"It's an excellent deal," said Carlton.

"For who?"

"For Keystone."

"Or for you?"

He scowled.

I scanned a few pages and looked at Carlton.

"So, you plan to steal Keystone?"

"Nonsense."

"That's what this document amounts to. Twelve per cent is an outrageously high interest rate."

"Keystone needs the money."

"But Participating Preference shares? That means your dividend would be payable first, before any dividend to the present owners. And Cumulative? What if the company can't pay and falls behind?"

"Then I could exercise my conversion rights."

"You could end up controlling the company."

"True."

"That's what I call stealing."

He ignored my remark. "Or I could force the

company into bankruptcy, in which my shares would take precedence."

"Well aren't you smart," I said. Bankruptcy is a sore subject with me.

He shrugged. "A lot of the venture capitalists are using this kind of stock."

"How does Quentin Teague come into this?"

Thunderclouds. "Keystone turned me down. Said they were talking to Teague."

So that was it. Hence the jealousy. Teague might not possess Carlton's analytical skills but on his home turf in London, he was well connected and a nearly unstoppable force. He was also not above playing the chauvinist card with references to ugly Americans.

There was the sound of a car arriving and in walked two young women, laughing. From their dress, they had been playing tennis.

One was Mimi, Carlton's wife, young enough at 25 to be his granddaughter. The other was my friend Kathy.

I got a kiss from each of them, which was nice, almost enough to make up for my annoyance with Kathy.

"What brings you here?" I asked her.

"Mimi wanted someone for tennis."

"And a chat," said Mimi.

"Besides, this is my area, sort of," said Kathy. "I live in Florida in case you had forgotten."

The women collapsed onto chairs. Both were wearing tennis skirts, so the amount of leg on display was generous. I found myself comparing the two. They shared a lively intelligence. Both were slim but not skinny, with good figures and healthy tans. Kathy was blonde and Mimi was dark. Other than that, they might be sisters.

I was not the only one enjoying the view. Carlton's grouchy manner had dissolved, giving way to an appreciative leer as he focused on their thighs. Kathy saw his gaze. Far from being annoyed she just shrugged.

"Your husband's a dirty old man," she said to Mimi.

"It's disgraceful," said Mimi.

They giggled.

"Not my fault if you dress like tarts," said Carlton. He did not seem embarrassed.

I felt we were straying off point.

"I'll take a look at Teague," I said to Carlton. "Are we done now? If so there's an earlier plane I can catch."

Carlton looked at Kathy. "Anything to add?"

She thought for a minute. "About Saddiq?"

"He's been arrested." I said. I was getting a bit

tired of having to explain things twice, first to Carlton and then to her.

"Yes," she said patiently. "I just wonder about the rest of his organization. He presumably has associates who know who you are."

Kathy has a way of complicating simple situations, slowing them down to a point where they become a tangled mess. It makes my job more difficult. She's often right, which makes her doubly annoying.

"I'll take my chances," I said.

"I did some research," she said. "There's a company called Saddiq Construction in Oran, a port in Algeria."

"So?"

"Saddiq is Algerian."

"It's a common Arabic name," said Carlton. "But she's right, you should keep your eyes open."

"Always," I said.

I left before they could think of anything else to slow me down, but I missed the early plane.

46

S addiq Construction's offices were in Oran, a major Algerian port. The company occupied a six-storey building, its dusty exterior plain but suggesting a substantial business.

The owner, Suleman al Saddiq, sat behind a large desk on the top floor. From his desk he could look out at several of his container ships in process of unloading.

A gaunt Arab in his fifties with sunken eyes in a lined face, black moustache framing downturned lips, he wore a white Arab robe but he spoke on the phone in fluent, rapid-fire French.

The photos on his office wall attested to the part Suleman had played in the country's prosperity. There were pictures of him shaking hands with political leaders, from Palestine leader Yasser Arafat to the king of Saudi Arabia. But there were no photos to indicate his other obsession, his support for Al Qaeda. That required total secrecy.

He was only five years old when Algeria gained independence from France. His father, a small businessman under the French colonists or *pieds noirs*, instilled in his son a hatred of foreign powers and a strong streak of anti-Semitism.

When Mustafa called from Los Angeles to tell him of his son Saddiq's arrest, Suleman was roused to fury. He ordered Mustafa to find out everything he could, and to keep a close watch on Oliver Steele.

Mustafa had no luck with the first task. The media did not report the events outside South Bay Squash Club and when he called Torrance Police, they denied all knowledge of the incident.

He had better luck tracing Oliver Steele. So Suleman knew of Oliver's departure for England and was able to arrange for an associate to pick up the trail at London's Gatwick Airport.

Suleman's orders to his colleague boiled down to a single word – revenge.

47

I arrived in Central London via a bumpy overnight flight to Gatwick, a train to Victoria Station and a cab ride to the Hyde Park Hotel, a five-star establishment with large, well heated rooms. My sixth-floor room overlooked the park.

After coffee and a shower I took the underground to Kings' Bench Walk, the site of many barristers' chambers. The names of the occupants are listed beside the doors and at No.3 I found Victor Aronson Q.C.

His name was at the top of a column of sixteen lawyers. A lady in a woolen cardigan showed me to his office. He got up from behind a leather-topped desk.

"Mr Steele." He motioned me to a settee.

Through mullioned windows I could see green grass in the courtyard outside.

Aronson was short and round. He surveyed me over half-moon spectacles.

"My friend Murray says you want to know about foreign trusts."

On the plane I had tried to read his book on offshore business centers. Despite the elegant writing, it had sent me to sleep. I showed him the names and numbers I had filched from Detective Gray.

He scanned it. "What were your party's objectives?"

To protect his assets from invasion, and keep them secret."

Aronson nodded. "He would probably have formed an asset protection trust."

"How does that work?"

"He would put his assets in a trust, controlled by the Trustee."

"So he would lose control?

"Actually no," said Aronson. "He would execute something called a Letter of Wishes. The letter spells out how the Trustee should manage the assets, although the Trustee is not obliged to comply."

"So the Trustee can disregard Mr. Kalestian's memorandum of wishes?"

"He wouldn't do that."

"Why not?"

"Because of another person, called the Protector. The Protector's only power is to fire the Trustee and appoint a new one."

"So Kalestian keeps control without appearing to have control? That's clever."

"That's how it works."

"One last thing." I produced Kalestian's list. "Where would these accounts be located, do you think?"

He smiled. "I don't get involved with opening bank accounts, I deliberately keep well clear of that. If it appeared that I was hiding money overseas, or even helping someone else to do so, my career would be over."

I got up to leave. "Thanks, anyway."

He said thoughtfully, "Some operators are not as scrupulous as we barristers. London has a large immigrant population with overseas connections. Some of them are more flexible."

"Where would I look for someone like that?"

"You could make enquiries in Southall."

I knew of Southall as an unfashionable suburb, seldom visited by tourists. My surprise must have shown, because he laughed.

"Why not go there and look around? Southall might surprise you."

48

I hailed a black cab. The driver was a wiry red-haired cockney.

"Where to, guv'nor?"

"Southall."

We rumbled past Hyde Park Corner, down Knighsbridge, west along Cromwell Road and eventually cruised down Southall High Street.

"What address?"

"Just drive slowly."

I felt as if I was in India. Indian shops, restaurants, banks. The Chinatown concept but Indian-style, in drab red brick. seasoned with London grime and dotted with stores like sequins on a shabby dress.

I had a plan but I needed a starting point. Spotting the black and silver shield of First Bank of

Commerce International, I paid off my taxi and went in.

It was a small branch with two service windows, one of them shut.

"Yes, sir?" A woman in a floral salwar kameez – tunic and long trousers – nodded at me.

"I want to open an offshore account."

"You need Mr. Patel." She called over her shoulder, "Naresh!"

A young Indian in a dark suit appeared. He shook hands without smiling, showed me into a tiny conference room and waited for me to speak.

"I have an import-export business. I need advice on setting up an account overseas."

He cut me short. "We don't do that kind of business unless you have extensive references."

"I'm sorry. I thought ..."

"We used to, but nowadays the bank has to be careful. We had some bad publicity."

"Can you can recommend anyone?"

A business card appeared, as if by magic. "Talk to this man."

I read. "Haresh Agha, solicitor." An address in the same street.

"He will help you."

He stood up. The meeting was over. I considered whether to take offense at being bundled out so fast, but decided against. Mr. Patel might be brusque but he had not wasted my time. I had what I wanted, an introduction.

I walked the three blocks to Agha's address. What I found was not a law office but a shop, 'Bargainstore Electronics.' It displayed a variety of gadgets, from video recorders to vibrators.

I asked for Mr Agha and was directed upstairs into a none-too-clean corridor with several wooden doors. One bore the legend "Haresh Agha, LLB and Partners," in do-it-yourself stick-on letters. I knocked.

"Come!"

Inside was a small Indian wearing a loud tweed suit in a hounds-tooth check more suited to race-track than office. He rose to his full height of five feet nothing and pumped my hand.

"Harry Agha. Sit ye down, sit ye down."

The office was bare, with a single metal filing cabinet in one corner. No sign of the partners promised on the door.

"So you want to open an offshore account?"

"Yes."

"No problem, Squire." Sharp eyes in his little round face flickered over me. "And you are, don't tell me, from America?"

"Yes."

"New York, Miami, LA?"

"Los Angeles."

"Wonderful city."

"Have you been there?"

"Not been there, but know of it, yes. My cousin has a restaurant in Beverly Hills."

He saw me looking around the plain room and laughed nervously.

"Low overhead, that's my watchword." But I noticed his suit fitted perfectly and must have cost a lot of money.

"Are you associated with the electronics company downstairs?" I was curious.

He laughed uproariously as though I had made a good joke. I waited for him to answer but he did not. I tried again.

"How did you know I wanted an offshore account?"

"My cousin called, didn't he?"

"Cousin?"

"Naresh Patel. Nice boy. No problem."

Cousins seemed to be part of his modus operandi.

He handed me some Xeroxed pages, stapled together. At the top in heavy type were the words "International Fiscal Services" and, below, "Offices Around the World." Then, a list of countries in which corporations could be formed, with a price for each.

I read that I could form a company in Belize for

only $200. Annual maintenance was also $200. The Cayman Islands were more expensive, $1,200 for setup and $750 for maintenance. A dozen other places were priced in between. Other services included opening bank accounts and providing nominee directors. It reminded me of the menu at an expensive restaurant.

He watched me. "We take credit cards," he said.

"Can you open bank accounts?"

"Yes sir."

"In which countries?"

"Any country, no problem." He waved airily.

I reached in my pocket, drew out my bankroll, peeled off $1,000 in fifties I handed them to him.

"I am retaining you as a consultant to set up an offshore banking facility. Here's an advance against the bill."

He took the money and looked at it. He seemed embarrassed.

"Excuse me for asking, squire, but what business did you say you were in?"

"Import export," I said.

"That wouldn't include drugs, would it?"

"Certainly not."

A smile spread over his chipmunk face and the notes disappeared inside his jacket. "Had to ask," he said.

Our relationship improved at that point, possibly

because I was now a client and not just a prospect. I found myself almost liking him.

I took Kalestian's list of accounts from my pocket.

"Can you tell, by looking, which bank these accounts belong to?"

He studied the list. "You mean, does the sequence of letters and numbers indicate a particular bank?"

I nodded.

"Could be several. Any one of dozens, to be honest."

"I need to know. I have $10,000 to deposit and one of those banks is where I want to put my money. Never mind why."

He nodded. "Understood, squire." He thought for a minute. "Hang about. Let's try something." He turned to the metal cabinet and opened a drawer to reveal rows of hanging folders. He selected one and studied its contents. Shook his head, replaced it and took out another. After a quarter of an hour, he had replaced a dozen files but had set three out on the desk.

"I can't show you these but they represent banks in three different countries." With a gold propelling pencil, he wrote on a notepad and pushed it across the desk.

"Could be any of these. The numbering sequence fits in each case."

In a neat fist, I read:

Bauer Privatbank *AG, Liechtenstein.*

Keystone Bank, *St. Lydia.*

Royal Bank of Selangor, *Kuala Lumpur, Malaysia.*

"Well, that narrows it within 8,000 miles," I said.

He looked crestfallen. I said hastily, "A big step forward, though. May I have this?"

"Be my guest, squire." He put his gold pencil away. "What next?"

I looked at my watch. It would soon be morning in Los Angeles and I wanted to check in with Clyde.

"I must get back to town. Is there an underground station nearby?"

He held up a hand in mock anger. "Out of the question, squire. Car's outside. I'll run you back."

"I don't want to trouble you." But Agha would have none of it. He led the way out of his office, locking it carefully. "Let's go out the back."

Downstairs he ushered me into a maroon Rolls Royce. It was immaculately polished and looked brand new. He trotted round to the driver's seat. His chin barely reached the bottom of the windscreen. Humming to himself, he guided us into traffic and headed north across the common.

I was surrounded by walnut, leather and expensive carpeting. "Lovely car," I said.

"Ho, yes, thank you. Eats up petrol, sorry to say but otherwise, not a bad runabout."

I got it. This was part of the image. Showing off the Roller had made his day.

As we drove through the City of London, the scene took me back to my days as a trainee accountant. The streets looked full of bored, depressed men and women trudging along in cheap suits.

At my request, Agha dropped me in Borough High Street, just south of London Bridge. I watched the Rolls out of sight, then bought a Financial Times and ducked into the George, an old Elizabethan coaching inn, for a sandwich and a Guinness.

With is pink pages and lapidary prose, the FT is an organ of international renown that reports in mind-numbing detail on the world's business.

The headline concerned a phone company merger. Two dapper chief executives were pictured shaking hands and beaming that smile that chief executives wear when neither is sure whose hand wields the bigger knife-in-the-back. I was about to turn to the Arts section when a headline caught my eye:

"TEAGUE BUYS BANKING GROUP"

Teague Holdings yesterday announced the agreed purchase of investment bank Keystone Guarantee. Terms were three Teague shares for each Keystone share.

Keystone offers private client banking, through branches on Jersey, Guernsey and St. Lydia in the Caribbean.

COMMENT: Teague fans may question the logic of an engineering group buying a private banking business, but Teague has successfully integrated past acquisitions. Teague shares are at an all-time high."

There was a photo of Quentin Teague beaming through his glasses.

Private banking in St. Lydia? Draining my Guinness, I hurried to a payphone and called Agha.

"International Fiscal Services."

"Oliver Steele here."

"Ho, yes. Just got back. Nice smooth run."

"Listen, it's the Keystone Bank."

"St. Lydia, eh? Nice little haven. Exclusive."

"Do you have a cousin there?"

"I have cousins everywhere, squire."

"That's where I want the account opened."

"Fair enough, sport. I'll draft the forms and fax them to your hotel."

I TOOK the underground back to the hotel. Far below my window, two trim horsewomen in black jackets and fawn jodhpurs were trotting their mounts round a bridle-track beneath the plane trees. Magda had arrived in London and her room was next to mine;

she had left a note under my door saying, 'Gone to the B.M. to tickle the Elgin Marbles.'

I dialed Clyde in California. "It's Oliver."

"Where are you?"

"London." I felt like Murrow in the Blitz. "Any messages?"

"Yeah. Some chick called from Monte Carlo. Works for Stanley Baxter. He really wants to meet you. Need the number?"

"I have it. What else?"

"Not much. Have fun, buddy."

I called Monte Carlo. A woman answered in French but immediately switched to English.

"Thanks for calling back, Mr. Steele, this is Leila Cavour, executive assistant to Mr. Baxter. He wants so much to see you."

"Put him on."

"He is . . . not here just now." She was good. Not perfect, but pretty good.

"I'll see how I'm fixed. I'm rather busy."

"Where are you, Mr. Steele?"

"In London. Maybe lunch tomorrow?"

"I'll check his diary."

I could hear her talking to the boss who was not there. She came back. "That's fine."

I called Air France. There was a 5pm flight to Nice. The underground runs straight from Knightsbridge to the airport, so I had some time. I strolled down the road and into Harrods where I sat at the lunch counter in the store's magnificently tiled food hall.

The place was full of business people of both genders, mostly in pinstripes. I ordered a slice of game pie and a bottle of Perrier – I usually ask for tap water but this was Harrods and I just didn't have the nerve. I was addressing my pie when someone took the empty seat beside me.

We smiled at each other. He was wearing the usual pinstripes. He was a smooth-faced, dark skinned fellow in his thirties, possibly Middle Eastern, which was not unusual. Half the world's visitors shop at Harrods when they come to London.

"Is that the game pie?" he asked. The trace of an accent.

I nodded.

"How is it?"

"Pretty good."

He looked at me thoughtfully. "A shame, because you will not have time to finish it."

The Food Halls can get noisy – something about the way the sound bounces off those lovely ceramic tiles, so I didn't hear what he said. Or just didn't process it.

But, looking at his face, I knew I was in trouble. The friendly smile had become a mask and in my ribs I felt what I assumed was a gun.

It's funny, after the business at the squash club I had been expecting trouble, but not in Harrods. It was an unfortunate lapse of imagination on my part because here was my nemesis, in bright light amid a well-heeled crowd.

The noise level would hide a silenced gunshot, after which this character could slip quietly away. He looked more thoughtful than Saddiq, and more professional.

"What happens now?"

"We go for a walk," he said. He produced a £50 note, more than enough for my food. "The meal's on me," he said. He left a generous tip.

As we left, he kept the gun pointing firmly my way.

Things looked bleak and I'm sure my new friend thought he had things under control. But I did have one card to play of which, it's safe to say, he had no inkling.

I am an Old Harrodian. When I was a student at Oxford, impoverished like most students, I did vacation work and one Christmas I worked at Harrods. I wore a white coat and sold cooked meats to the public. I almost sold a pork pie to the Queen Mother when she came by with the owner. She smiled charmingly and moved on. No sale, but a big day for me.

So I knew about the underground world of

Harrods, the complex network of passages beneath our feet. It connected all the unseen departments – the cold store, the goods entrances, the staff elevators and canteen and so on. Behind many of the sales counters, un-noticed by customers, there were steps leading down to these tunnels. Down those steps, I hoped, lay safety.

I glanced around. It had been a few years and I had forgotten some of the geography. But I knew what I was looking for. From the lunch counter, the nearest steps down to the tunnels were behind the lambs' fries counter in the butchers shop. Lambs' fries are lambs' testicles, much favoured, surprisingly, by genteel ladies living in Basil Street and Cadogan Square. They are said to be delicious in a cream sauce although personally I could never bring myself to try them. Fortunately the fries were still in the same place and we were heading that way.

The key was to behave calmly – employees were used to seeing other employees pass through the staff doors, so there was nothing unusual about a neatly dressed individual doing that.

I took a deep breath and, in mortal fear of a bullet in the back, put my faith in the element of surprise. As we reached the offal counter, before my companion knew what was happening, I stepped quickly aside and vanished, shutting the door behind me.

It was quiet down there and I enjoyed a moment of calm. There was a street sign, just as there is on any street. I was standing on Cold Store Avenue and I remembered that it led into Burbidge Way, named after a distinguished past chairman. Burbidge Way was a straight tunnel, about 80 yards long, leading past staff toilets and terminating at the staff entrance at the Hyde Park end of the store. I set out at a trot.

I had not expected my pursuer to be easily shaken off and sure enough, as I rounded the corner onto Burbidge Way, I heard running feet. It could be a Harrods employee hurrying to get to the bathroom, but I didn't think so.

I ducked into the toilets, out of sight of my pursuer. At the last moment I stepped out to confront him. No firearm visible, so I assumed it was in his pocket.

By this point, frankly, I was angry. I threw a right-hand punch and my fist sank into his stomach. He gasped as the air left his lungs. Before he could get his breath, I wound an arm round his neck, tightened my grip and held on until I was sure he was unconscious.

When I felt his body relax, I wrestled him back into the bathroom which, thankfully, was empty. I tugged him into a stall and arranged his body on the white china pedestal. He sagged forward and I nudged his body to and fro until it achieved some sort of equilibrium.

I felt his wrist for a pulse but could not find one. I am no medic but at that moment I realized with a jolt that I had killed him.

Decision time. Should I call for help, and stay around to deal with the consequences? Or exit Harrods in a hurry?

Not a hard choice. He had been about to kill me. Instead, I had killed him.

No remorse. What I did do was to take a slip of paper, some kind of cash receipt, from my pocket, fold it in a wedge and jam it into the lock of the stall so that when I slammed the door it would stay shut, hopefully delaying the next use of the stall.

It was only as I left that I saw I had been in the ladies' and not the men's toilets.

49

I left Harrods by the staff entrance, walked the few steps to Knightsbridge Underground station and bought a ticket. Moments later I was just an innocent traveller sitting in a Piccadilly line train as it rumbled its way out to the airport.

I made the flight easily and, 90 minutes later, landed at Nice. I rented a Citroen the size of a sardine can and drove east, taking the scenic route along the Moyenne Corniche, the middle of the three roads that cling to the coastal mountains. The little car hugged every twist and turn on the way to Monaco.

As I approached the principality, the sun was setting over the Mediterranean, bathing expensive villas and old fishing villages alike in its glow. The breeze wafted scents of sage and rosemary into the car and by the time I negotiated the hairpin bends down into Monte Carlo, my seduction by the Riviera was complete. I had needed to relax after speeding along freeways and sprinting through Harrods like a wind-up toy, and the region's soothing influence did its work.

Somerset Maugham famously described Monte Carlo as a sunny place for shady people. Now a tax haven for rock stars and tennis players, it is also home to the mother of all casinos which was something I wanted to see.

I would have checked into the Hotel de Paris, considered by many to be the best hotel in town – standard operating procedure when working for Carlton – but I was feeling a bit anti-Carlton, a mood that comes over me sometimes, so instead I chose the very civilised Hotel Hermitage, a few blocks away. From there I strolled to the Casino.

It stood floodlit in the dusk. The belle époque façade shone like gold, an extravaganza of ornate towers and stained glass windows framed by palm trees. Men in dinner jackets and women in smart dresses mounted its steps, laughing and chatting.

A white-haired man in his seventies, eyes watery in hollow cheeks, tottered up the steps. He was wearing a linen jacket, white but yellowing, and his tie – black silk with thin blue stripes – was sloppily tied, the narrow end longer than the wide. He looked British: a remittance man getting monthly checks from the family trust to stay out of England?

An Arab stepped out of a black limousine, a desert hawk, his face lean and tanned, beard gleaming, black cloak trimmed with gold. He ignored the commissionaire who held the car door open and swept into the building in an aura of wealth. I expected a retinue to follow him but there was just one man in western dress looking like a secretary, mild faced and slim. I followed them inside.

The lobby was elegant and much different from Las Vegas. Where Las Vegas imitated style, this building defined it. White walls supported gilt framed mirrors; crystal chandeliers hung from coffered ceilings. The staff wore black dinner jackets. Now and then a smile would split one of their faces.

I played a few hands of blackjack to get the feel of things. I even won a hundred euros – a lot for me. Then I ordered a Pernod and drifted into one of the other rooms. Sipping my drink, I watched some baccarat. I recognized the Arab from outside – he had the bank and a pile of chips at his elbow.

Baccarat has an aura of excitement about it, due to the wagering rather than to any skill needed. The players have few judgments to make. They just bet, either with or against the bank. The cards are dealt – two cards per hand – one hand to the banker and another to each player. Depending on the point count, a third card may be dealt. The winning hand is the one scoring closest to nine points.

The stakes were high. The popular chip was 200 euros – more than I had won all evening – and players were betting five and ten chips. Several were betting heavily against the bank and losing.

As I watched, a large man in his fifties and a young woman arrived and the man sat down to play. He had a booming voice that carried above the general noise and seemed to be making a big deal out of his own arrival.

"Champagne, garçon! Let's get organized here." He spoke English but clearly expected to be understood. The dealer pushed a pile of chips towards him but no money passed – presumably he had credit.

"You may deal now," he said. It was hard to tell if he was joking or just pompous. He was heavily built, with a huge gut masked by expensive tailoring. His face was red and blotchy and his jowls hung like a bloodhound's, dark with five o'clock shadow. He kept up a running commentary, clearly irritating his neighbors. Suspicion as to his identity began to dawn on me.

The woman stood behind him, her hands on his shoulders. She looked thin and fragile in a black cocktail dress with no jewellery. I could count her vertebrae. Most women dressed like that would have seemed plain but she carried it off and was drawing looks from the bystanders. She had huge eyes with a sadness about them, unless it was my imagination working overtime.

For half an hour the big newcomer won more than he lost. Meanwhile, the Arab's pile was shrinking and his face was becoming less hawk-like and more unhappy. At one point he retrieved the bank and won a few hands. Then the newcomer began to bet heavily against him and win. An audience gathered.

As I ordered another drink, I caught the eye of my neighbor. It was the man in the linen jacket. Close up, he looked even more watery-eyed and I guessed he was slightly drunk. He nodded at me.

"That's Sidney Baxter."

"I wondered," I said. "Is he here often?"

"Whenever he's in town. They say he's addicted, although I've not seen it and I'm here a lot."

"How does one recognise a gambling addict?"

"Good question. Maybe it's anyone who plays until he runs out of money." Linen Jacket drained his martini. "A bit like an alcoholic who goes on drinking until the bottle is empty."

I bought him another.

"Thanks, old boy." He warmed to his subject. "Of course, if you're Baxter, you don't run out of money."

"Is he that rich?"

My companion snorted. "Ten billion, I hear."

"Dollars?"

"Pounds. He plays high-stakes blackjack with Baggott and the Chinese boys."

"Do they play here?"

"The Chinese?" He shook his head. "They prefer Las Vegas. Can't think why. Dreadful place." He sniffed.

"Been there, have you?" I asked.

"Certainly not. Wouldn't be seen dead. Monte for me. I'm Quigly, by the way." He stuck out a hand.

"Steele."

I added after a pause "I'm guessing you're English."

He nodded. "Lincolnshire. Never go there now, too chilly. You American?"

"Half. English mother, American father. I live in California."

"Thought so. Must be the tailoring."

"So is Baxter slumming tonight? I see he's playing for a paltry €1,000 a hand."

Quigly wagged a cautionary finger. "Things may get interesting later. Keep an eye on the Arab."

"I've been watching. He seems to have lost most of his chips."

Quigly snorted. "Not him, the other one."

I looked but could only see one Arab.

Quigly noticed my confusion. "Chap beside him."

The man on the Arab's left was clean-shaven and wore western clothes. I had seen him entering the casino in the wake of his flamboyant colleague but had not given him a second glance.

"Who is he?"

"Just watch."

The bearded Arab had the bank at this point. He was down to a few thousand euros and still losing.

In baccarat, a player can call "Banco" at any time, at which his bet is registered in an amount equal to the whole of the banker's remaining balance. This sets up a confrontation between player and banker and if the banker loses he cedes the bank.

As we watched, Baxter called "Banco." The dealer dealt two cards to Baxter and two to the Arab. Baxter's cards were a four and a five – a natural nine. The bank drew two nines, a total of eighteen. In baccarat only the last digit of the total counts, so that was an eight-point hand, losing to Baxter's nine. The bank was cleaned out.

The Arab stood up in disgust. Apparently unable to continue, he stepped back from the table.

Baxter beamed and took over the bank. He shot his cuffs and smiled over his shoulder at the girl.

"Out of his depth," he said.

The Arab flushed and turned away.

It was a rude remark and I marked Baxter down

as a poor winner. I wondered if he was an equally poor loser.

Baxter's chips continued to pile up until he had more than $60,000. He grew louder, oblivious to the irritation of the other players. The dealer watched expressionless as play continued.

At the last moment before dealing began, someone uttered the word "Banco" so quietly that it was not immediately clear who had said it. Baxter looked round in surprise. It was the Arab's quiet companion.

"Ah, a challenge," boomed Baxter. He glanced at the player's chips. "I see you have the wherewithal."

As it turned out, Baxter won the hand. The player watched, seemingly unconcerned, as his substantial bet was scooped in and moved over to Baxter's side of the table. On the next hand, he called "banco" again. Baxter won again. He now had close to $240,000 piled up in front of him. A crowd started to gather.

"Better luck next time, sir," rumbled Baxter, smiling.

The other player's chips were nearly gone. I expected him to leave, or at least back away. Instead, he signaled to the pit boss. A nod sufficed; the player took out a check book and wrote a check which he slid across to the dealer. As I watched, chips worth half a million dollars were counted out and pushed towards him.

He again called "Banco," his face as calm as before.

For the first time, Baxter looked disconcerted. It was probably dawning on him that he stood to lose his entire accumulation. Surprise gave way to irritation. He turned his massive head towards the slightly built player, eying him like a lion appraising his next meal.

The player appeared not to notice. The cards were dealt.

The banker drew a six and a two, making eight. Not a perfect score, but only one short of it. Baxter was dealt a seven and a queen; face cards count for zero, so this gave him a score of seven. Since this was a loser to the bank's eight, he drew. The three of clubs gave him ten and he lost.

The dealer raked Baxter's chips together and pushed them over to the other player, who now had well over half a million dollars.

Baxter's fist thumped the green tabletop. "This is absurd!" The table was solidly built, but it shook. A hush fell. Even to a French-speaking audience, his anger was clear.

"More chips, dealer."

The dealer hesitated, apparently unclear as to

precisely what the request meant. He looked to his pit boss for guidance. The pit boss approached. The two men conferred in lowered voices. The pit boss walked round the table to where Baxter sat and spoke in his ear.

If he had meant to respect Baxter's privacy he could have saved himself the walk. The big man exploded.

"What do you mean, no arrangement? This is ridiculous."

The pit boss was respectful but firm. "It is understood. But monsieur's limit has been reached."

I was not surprised. If Baxter wanted to challenge the bank, he would probably need half a million dollars to do it.

"Then we need a new arrangement."

The French may be experts on love but they are also quite sharp when it comes to money. Money talks but its absence can generate a deafening silence.

The pit boss stood his ground, shrugging well-tailored shoulders. He looked deferential but adamant.

Baxter glared. "I repeat, a new arrangement is required. Where's the manager?"

The duty manager was called. Discussions took place, loud on Baxter's part, respectful by the manager. They seemed to be making little progress. I heard muttered references by management to "formalities" and "vingt-quatre heures" – twenty-four hours. Was he telling Baxter they must check his credit before he could play on? Strange. If he was as rich as people said, he should be good for it. And the casino had accepted the other player's check for half a million without hesitation. What was I missing?

I turned to Quigly, who was smiling.

"What's the joke?"

"Just watch."

Finally, Baxter pushed back his chair and heaved himself to his feet. His bulk quivering, he faced the impassive player opposite and shook a fist in the man's face. His expression was mean. At that moment, it did not seem fanciful to think of him as a murderer.

"I am leaving, but we shall meet again. And when we do, I shall break you, do you hear?"

He turned and strode away, his female companion in tow.

They got as far as the door. The girl was talking animatedly, hurrying to keep up. He slowed and then stopped, bending his head to listen.

Suddenly his rage seemed to fade, replaced by thoughtfulness. He turned and re-approached the table, where play had resumed. He was wearing what is technically known as a shit-eating smile.

"Your Highness, it's been a privilege to play at the same table as you."

The change from hostile to obsequious was complete. He was literally fawning. It was as if the previous rage had never occurred. I would have been embarrassed for him, except that he himself was obviously incapable of embarrassment.

The player stared back, in surprise.

"My name is Baxter, sir. You may have seen my yacht, the Guinevere."

The player nodded – anything else would have been boorish.

"Let me give you my card sir." Baxter patted his pocket but found no card. He snapped at his companion "Leila, give his Highness a card." Leila complied.

"People say my chef is the best in Europe. I hope to have the pleasure of entertaining you – and your companion of course" – he nodded at the berobed Arab who was eyeing him like a piece of camel dung on the heel of his boot. Baxter stood there for a full minute, his ingratiating smile fixed. Finally, he seemed to realise he was no longer welcome. He bowed awkwardly, turned and left, his elegant squaw following a few steps behind.

I turned to Quigly. "You've made your point. Now, who's the other player?"

He laughed. "That's the Emir of Ras al Doha."

"Of where?"

"One of the Trucial states in the Persian Gulf."

"And his magnificent companion?"

Quigly shrugged. "Nobody. A bodyguard."

"The Emir is pretty well-heeled?"

"He owns every barrel of oil underneath his particular patch of sand. Some say he's the richest man in the world."

"So Mr Baxter's threat to break him was over-ambitious?"

"A little."

"Surely the casino could extend Baxter's credit."

Quigly grinned. "Maybe they prefer to earn brownie points with the Emir. That's the French for you."

"But Baxter is pretty rich himself."

"Depends what you mean. There's rich and there's rich. Baxter's wealth is on paper – stock in his own company. Its value fluctuates. In a big crash he could even be wiped out. The Emir's wealth, on the other hand, is secure. The world needs oil. There's no way he could be threatened financially."

"You seem to know a bit about all this."

Quigly hesitated, as if there were things he did not want to reveal to a stranger. Then he laughed.

"My family is in banking; I grew up hearing

about that stuff." He stuck out a hand. "That's it for me . . . don't lose too much." He tottered away.

I soon followed suit. I had gained some insight about my host for lunch tomorrow. It had been a long day. When my head hit the pillow, I went out like a light.

50

Next morning I slept late, then breakfasted on the hotel terrace. Afterwards I walked in bright sunshine to the Condamine area where the yachts are. I was to be met at eleven thirty by the Guinevere's launch.

I was early, so I strolled along the quay admiring the yachts whose sterns aligned in a neat row against the jetty. On one of them, a white jacketed steward was placing folded napkins in wine glasses and straightening silverware. In the middle of the table were a bowl of fruit and a basket of rolls. I was strongly tempted to walk up the teak gangway and sit down. This was no place for the budget-conscious – I estimated the yachts averaged about fifty tons, their ports of origin ranging from Piraeus to Rio de Janeiro.

With a throaty rumble, a small launch drew up and a wiry seaman in white shirt and shorts hailed me. "Signor Steele?"

"That's me."

"Please to come for the Guinevere."

He helped me aboard. With a surge of power the little craft roared away from the dock and out to sea. We threaded our way between even bigger yachts at anchor. Most of them seemed deserted. I wondered who got to moor close to shore, rather than in open water. Was it like a restaurant where the attendant parks the Ferrari and the Porsche out front and relegates your Ford to parking Siberia?

My driver was Italian. He replied to my conversational efforts with a baffled smile. I amused myself by speculating which yacht was the Guinevere. I assumed it would be at least as big as the sixty footers moored at the dock – Baxter's girth would require no less. I eliminated several candidates before realising our destination was the sleek juggernaut half a city block long. It had its own floating jetty, shaded by a canvas awning. I knew there would be a swimming pool and probably a ballroom as well.

Baxter was there to greet me, standing at the top of the gangway.

"Welcome aboard, Mr Steele."

He pumped my hand vigorously and roared with

laughter, his mirthless eyes nestling in layers of flesh.

He wore a peaked yachting cap, white trousers and rope-soled espadrilles. His huge belly was barely contained by a matelot's striped singlet. If it was supposed to make him look nautical, it failed.

"First time aboard my beauty, eh? Shall we take the tour?" He clapped a bear-like arm round my shoulders and we were off.

I counted a dozen staterooms. 'Cabins' hardly did them justice - they were about the size of the guest cottages at Hearst's castle. The shore-side windows had a panoramic view of Monte Carlo and the Casino, set against a heat-hazed backdrop of high-rise apartment buildings and, beyond them, the mountains.

"Come on, come on." He was like a child in a nouveau-riche family, anxious to show that his toys cost more than your toys.

"Here's the galley. This is my chef, Sebastian." He pronounced it 'Sebastianne,' rolling the n with gusto. The large kitchen was a treasure house of stainless steel euipment. Sebastian, a slender blond with a pout, was doing something with a knife to a glistening fish. He waved a flour-covered hand but otherwise ignored us. We moved on.

"I bought her from Costas, the shipping fellow.

Had her refitted, of course. Here's the pool." We rounded the corner into sunlight.

Leila Cavour lay flat on her back wearing sunglasses and a bikini bottom, navy with white polka dots, her perfect chest offered up to the sun. She was rubbing her stomach lazily with Ambre Solaire. She smiled without removing the glasses.

"This is Mr. Steele, my dear," boomed Baxter."

She extended a hand to be shaken. It was moist with suntan oil. I like to think my hand remained steady.

"We spoke on the phone," she said.

"Yes."

"Come along, lots to see. Leila will join us for lunch," said Baxter. He was starting to get on my nerves, but it was his boat.

He marched me through the engine room, the bridge and yes, the ballroom. The yacht's designer had incorporated a parquet dance floor big enough for a small chateau. It stretched across the ship with windows on either side. Like most empty ballrooms it looked a bit sad, but Baxter was oblivious to such nuances.

Now and then we passed seamen. Baxter greeted them with a self-conscious smile and a hand raised to his peaked cap with a "Carry on, er . . ." as if he really wanted to remember their names. Their response was wary. I didn't know whether to credit him for good intentions or be appalled by his lack of empathy.

Finally he sat us down in reclining chairs on the after deck. A steward poured champagne – Baxter drank it like lemonade – and I sensed he was ready to make a pitch.

"I want those papers, Mr. Steele." His brows knitted like a boxer's. No more bonhomie.

"What papers?"

"I think you know." Black eyes bored into me.

"The question is, how did *you* know?"

"Don't bandy words with me." I sensed menace, or was it just the Czech showing through? It was a bit unnerving to be on his boat, surrounded by his people and some way from land. So far I had been running on adrenalin, fear alarms suspended, but now I started to feel anxious.

"I'm serious," I said, keeping my voice steady. "I have a job to do. I need some information. When I get it, it will tell me that someone – it may be you – killed Ara Kalestian."

He blinked. "I am not a murderer, I am a businessman, a very successful one. When one is successful, one does not need to do such things."

I wasn't sure I agreed. Successful businessmen can lie like a rug. Was he lying now?

He returned to the attack. "You only have shreds of information. They are no use to you."

"Don't be so sure."

"One can't walk into a bank and draw out $400 million. You need identification, introductions. You have none of that. You are nobody. The Game on the other hand, has been prepared, tested and rehearsed. It was ready to go, until something went wrong."

"What?"

His face looked thunderous. "One of the players broke the rules."

The waiter appeared. "Shall I serve lunch, sir?"

"Yes. Ask Miss Cavour to join us."

We moved to a table in the shade. Leila had put on her top, but she removed her sunglasses as she sat down. I was surprised to get a grin and a wink as Baxter fussed over the meal. The centerpiece was a whole sea bass grilled with fennel. Baxter's claims for his chef were correct. It was impeccable. I could have used a glass of Chablis but there was only champagne.

Baxter made light conversation during the meal but, over coffee, he returned to the subject of money.

He summarized the progress of the Game. He spoke freely in front of Leila. The project had been funded a year ago, when Kalestian began considering possible targets. He started by looking at US aid money allegedly stolen from the Philippines, and some of the more outrageous 'Savings and Loan' scandals in the United States. Other situations involved various dictators and embezzlers but he eventually narrowed the search down to ex-President Marcos.

The situation was complicated by a mess of lawsuits. There were intriguing differences between the amounts stolen and the amounts that could be traced to banks. These unexplained shortfalls were what fascinated Kalestian and inspired him to probe further.

"How did he plan to get his hands on the money?" I asked.

Baxter grinned wolfishly. "He cultivated former courtiers of President Marcos in the hope of persuading one to collaborate with him. It was a clever strategy and it worked."

Baxter explained how, basically using blackmail, Ara had persuaded the younger Raoul Cerdan to cooperate in exchange for a large bribe. At the appointed time, Cerdan would play his part in a carefully planned approach to the bank but, until then, his anonymity had to be preserved.

Baxter leaned forward and prodded my chest with a meaty finger.

"Those notes of yours identify the bank account in question. They are the last piece of the puzzle."

"Let's see if I understand," I said. "Whoever had

Kalestian killed was planning to cut in and scoop the pool, leaving the other players empty handed?"

"Yes. It's disgraceful!"

"Well I guess I've acquired a document worth $400 million," I said.

"To which you are not entitled. You're not a player."

"What difference does that make?"

"$2 million," he said coldly.

"Oh, you mean your $2 million ante? I see your point. But in which court did you plan to sue me?"

He changed tack. "Let's be reasonable. I know I speak for all the players when I say we can reach agreement."

I wondered briefly what it would be like to own $20 million. I got there by calculating five percent of $400 million. Why not?

He read my mind. "You could earn a lot of money."

"I'll think about it."

Leila, listening, looked surprised. Had she expected me to reject the bribe? Maybe she didn't share Baxter's murky ethics.

He looked at his watch. "Okay, but not for long. You may stay here if you wish."

"Until tomorrow?"

He nodded. "Leila, tell Sebastian we shall be one more for dinner."

51

I spent a pleasant afternoon by the pool, working on my tan and making small talk to the decorative Leila.

Two executives from Baxter's newspaper group arrived for dinner. They were clever and energetic. They laughed loudly at Baxter's jokes and flattered him ad nauseam.

He was drinking heavily. I estimated he put away a whole bottle of champagne at dinner. He had drunk most of a bottle at lunch. That would take its toll on most people but Baxter's words, although as bombastic as ever, did not become slurred.

The executives were not invited to spend the night. The launch took them ashore around ten o'clock. I went back to my cabin and read for a while. Then, in need of fresh air, I left my cabin and

wandered Guinevere's deserted decks, silent apart
from the subdued smack of waves against the steel
hull. Any street noise from Monte Carlo was carried
inland rather than out to sea.

I became aware of splashing astern. I strolled aft
in time to see a wet-suited rear end disappear underwater, followed by slim legs and flippers. As the
surface calmed, I could see a light moving around
underwater, then darker patches separating and
coalescing, playing tricks with my eyes. A seal-like
form surfaced, shook its head and swam towards a
ladder attached to the hull. It was Leila, with a flash-
light on a strap around her head.

She pushed her goggles up. "Give me a hand." I
took her arm and helped her up. The steel tank and
the weights round her waist probably added thirty
pounds to her slim frame but she handled them
deftly. She leaned against me, her arm on my
shoulder and shrugged off the buoyancy vest
supporting the heavy tank. Setting it down, she
unzipped her wetsuit. She wore a modest one-piece
bathing suit underneath.

"Come for a swim," she said.

Why not? I went back to the cabin and donned a
swimsuit but when I emerged, the diving gear had
vanished and so had its owner. I dived in and swam a
hundred yards towards the lights on shore, then
turned on my back and counted the stars, enjoying

the silence. After a while I swam slowly back and climbed on board.

There was nobody to be seen. I went back to my cabin and showered.

When I came out of the bathroom, she was there, wearing a short robe. Her wet hair was brushed straight and she looked ten years younger than the sophisticated beauty in the Casino.

She reached out and turned off the light, leaving moonlight filtering in through the window. She came and put her hands on my shoulders. I put my arms around her waist and kissed her.

Later she lay on her side and idly ran a fingernail across my chest.

"I know nothing about you," I said.

"You do now."

"You know what I mean. For instance, where do you come from?"

"I was born in Beirut. My family are Lebanese but I have an American passport."

"How so?"

"We left Lebanon when I was five. My father owned real estate in Beirut but when the fighting started, the city was devastated. He lost everything."

"But you got away?"

She nodded. He spent the last of his Lebanese pounds flying us to New York, on round-trip tickets.

"Round trip?"

"We had tourist visas. We knew Immigration would ask if we had tickets home. Once we were in America we threw away the return halves."

"And you got permanent visas later?"

"Eventually there was some sort of amnesty. Now we are Americans, respectable members of the middle class."

"You'll be telling me you went to an Ivy League university?"

She shook her head. "No. My brother did – he graduated from Harvard Law School. I went to San Diego to study marine biology at UCSD."

"That explains your diving skills, but why are you working for a charming fellow like Baxter?"

A pause. I could not see her face in the shadows.

"Is it my turn to ask questions yet?" she asked.

"Fire away."

"Why are you here?"

"What do you mean?"

"I don't think you're after the money."

"True. I've felt tempted, though."

"So what do you really want?"

"I need to know which of those four players flipped."

"Flipped?"

"Gave way to temptation. Hired a hit man to murder Kalestian and steal his list."

"You sound as if this is becoming personal."

"Perhaps. I may be a target too."

She was silent.

"Was it Baxter?" I asked.

More silence.

Then, "Can I trust you?"

"I don't know. Can you?"

"You asked why I work for Baxter. It's complicated. It involves my brother, who is a lawyer with a big firm in New York"

"He must be smart."

"He is, and he has a bright future. But two years ago there was a near-scandal. It involved insider trading. Word got round that Baxter was buying his own stock and not telling the SEC. If true, it would have destroyed the stock price."

"Was it true?"

"Yes. He was too smart to do it in his own name, but he devised a scheme involving offshore shell companies. They would borrow from foreign banks against the security of Baxter stock and use the money to buy more."

"Is that legal?"

"I don't know. The point is that it was undetectable, at least without an investigation that would have taken years. Baxter got away with it, as he always does."

"How was your brother involved?"

"It was his idea. They met at a dinner and, after a

few drinks, Aaron roughed out the scheme on a napkin. It was silly of him, but he thought it was just a joke."

"Don't tell me. Baxter was not joking?"

"Exactly. He kept the napkin. He threatened to destroy Aaron's good name if Aaron did not confirm publicly that no such scheme existed."

"Still could, I suppose?"

She nodded.

"Then I met Baxter at a seminar. The next day, he called and said he needed an assistant. He referred to the napkin incident and made it clear he would not take no for an answer. So, here I am."

"Don't you hate him?"

"Let's just say I don't forget."

We lay side by side. I don't know what was passing through her mind but eventually she spoke.

"He keeps notes."

"What sort of notes?"

"About the Game. In his office."

"That, I would like to see."

"I can take you there."

"Okay," I said. "But first I need to get something straight."

"Yes?"

"You and Baxter. I'm a bit slow-witted, so explain this to me. I saw you at the Casino last night. He escorts you. You spend a lot of time together. He has a large double bed."

She shook with laughter.

"No, I'm just one of his trophies. I'm also what they call a beard."

"Explain that."

"Ever wonder where the chef sleeps?"

I pictured Sebastian with his sulky face and wavy blond hair. I hadn't made the connection. Leila got out of bed and put on her robe. "Let's go for a walk."

We crept along the corridor and past Baxter's cabin.

"Won't we wake him?" I whispered.

"Not a chance. He'll sleep until dawn – you saw how much he drank."

"Is that normal for him?"

"Absolutely."

"What about Sebastian?"

"What about him?"

"What if he spots us?"

She snorted. "That self-absorbed tramp is incapable of any thought not involving himself. He'll assume we're playing some kind of sex game."

She stopped at a door. The lock had a numeric pad and she keyed in a code.

"This is Baxter's office."

She closed the door behind us and went over to the desk. Opening a drawer, she produced a file. I leafed through it. The contents were arranged in date order and, near the top, I found what I was looking for.

It was a copy of a fax that Baxter had sent to a Los Angeles number a week ago – before my visit to Murray Segal's office and before Ara Kalestian's death. It was in Baxter's florid style and I could almost hear him dictating it:

"<u>Most Confidential</u>:

Kalestian keeps information about the Game with his tax accountant, Segal. He will meet Segal on Saturday. He will bring back banking details to be revealed to the players in Las Vegas. Pray keep in mind that this information must NOT, repeat NOT reach the other players."

The implication was clear. The best way to stop information reaching the other players was to silence Kalestian.

52

I turned to Leila.

"This is the smoking gun. It's what I need."

"You can't take it away," she said.

I looked around. There was the usual office equipment, a computer, a copier and so on. "Is that a fax machine?"

"Yes."

I fed the memo into the input tray.

"What's the code for U.S.A?"

"Dial 001 and then the area code."

I entered Clyde's fax number and pushed 'Send.'

In a few seconds the page would reproduce itself electronically on Clyde's fax machine six thousand miles away in Los Angeles. He would be puzzled, but I would call him later to explain.

I took the original out of the fax machine and

returned it carefully to its place in the folder. "Let's get out of here."

Outside, she looked at me. "What next?"

"We could always go back to what we were doing before," I said.

She thought for a moment.

"Okay."

LEILA WAS GENTLY SHAKING ME. She was dressed. The sky was pre-dawn grey. A lone gull circled and dipped outside the window.

"Get up," she said. "Time to leave."

"What?"

"I'll take you ashore."

I checked my watch. "It's only five o'clock."

"Trust me."

I could have used some coffee but trusting her had worked so far. I got dressed.

Motioning me to silence, she cast off and drifted fifty yards from the Guinevere before starting the engine. Businesslike in jeans and navy sweater, her face expressionless, she guided us to shore. On the dock, she gave me a quick hug.

"Don't linger in Monte Carlo. Get out of town, and fast."

"Is Baxter onto me?"

She frowned, deflecting the question. "There are

things you don't need to know. Take my word, time is short."

"You're talking in riddles." I let my irritation show.

"Read tomorrow's newspaper."

As she guided the launch away, I got a dismissive wave, her back turned.

Dawn was breaking over a glassy ocean. A baker's boy cycled past with a load of baguettes. I walked back to the hotel through cool streets starting to come alive.

Before leaving my room, I phoned Magda in London. At the Hyde Park Hotel, the operator's English voice made me yearn for some old-fashioned Anglo-Saxon normality, after a mess of Czech ego and Levantine conspiracy.

I got a sleepy, "Do you know what the time is?"

"In Monaco it's 6am."

"You woke me up."

"We need to make plans."

"Did you find anything?"

"Yes. Baxter is the one who hired Zafi to kill Ara Kalestian."

"How do you know?"

"I have proof." I did not name my source. I didn't need the ribbing that would have followed, even at that hour, from Magda.

"Does he know you know?"

"I'm not sure. But he knows where the money is, or soon will."

"Did you tell him?"

"No. But take my word for it."

It was in the Financial Times, after all. Quentin Teague had shown his hand and if it was public knowledge that he had just bought a bank in the Caribbean, Baxter would put two and two together. He would, at the very least, suspect the account was there.

But he would still need the account number. That left me personally at risk.

Magda was starting to wake up. She said, "Teague is on his way to St. Lydia. Probably there by now."

"How do you know?"

"I called his office. Said I was his Australian stockbroker."

"How do you know he has a broker in Australia?"

"I don't. But neither does his upper-class secretary, who is as thick as two planks."

I could see an intercontinental foot race developing between Teague and Baxter. Each had cards to play. Teague owned the bank. Baxter knew about the shadowy Raoul. The other two players, Carlton Tisch and Louise Chang, seemed to be out of the running.

I didn't know how things would play out, but I knew where the action would be.

"Better pack your tropical kit."

"More airplanes?"

"Afraid so."

"Will you come to London first?"

"I don't think so. France has direct flights to the Caribbean. Do me a favour and find me somewhere to stay on St. Lydia."

"Any special hotel?"

"The best. We only use the best." I still had not had my coffee, and was feeling light-headed.

She paused long enough to let me know I was being childish.

"A bientôt," she said.

"See you in St. Lydia."

53

The morning Airbus to Paris was full of serious-faced businessmen. Not unlike the New York-DC shuttle, but with better cut suits. An occasional beret but fewer button-down shirts. The coffee was tepid but it got me to Charles de Gaulle in time to board UTA's daily jumbo to Martinique.

As the big jet floated up over the meadows of Brittany and headed west across the Atlantic, the sky turned from cloudy to blue. Sunlight flooded the half-empty cabin and the stewards seemed cheerful at having a manageably small payload. I ate coq au vin off good china and sipped coffee and Calvados as I scanned Paris Match, using my patchy French. Between that and a movie, nine hours later we reached Martinique.

The air seemed warmer than in the South of France – humid enough to carry the day's warmth into the evening, island rum rather than French champagne.

People still stroll in the islands, not like in the big cities where they stride, resolute and frowning, to their next appointment. A customs officer in tunic and shorts beckoned me over. He nodded politely. "Will you be with us long, Monsieur?"

"I'm en route to St. Lydia."

"A pleasant island, that one." He waved me through and I headed for the departure lounge which was a verandah with a few benches.

My next plane was an island-hopper with six seats and only three passengers. It rattled alarmingly. I stared down at white-beached islets as we approached St. Lydia.

The Frangipani Inn was a long, low arrangement of cedar bungalows round a central lobby and restaurant, facing its own curve of beach and flanked by palm groves. I was assigned a simple but well-appointed cabin. Through the window I could see yachts wheeling in the bay. There was serene silence. Magda had chosen well.

Now that I knew Sidney Baxter was responsible for Kalestian's death, my plan was threefold:

First, Sidney Baxter must be brought to justice.

The 'smoking gun' memo linking Baxter to Zafi should suffice but, with an army of lawyers at his beck and call, it would probably take time to put the ponderous publisher behind bars.

Second, Zafi had to be stopped before he killed me or anyone else.

Third, I wanted to find the money. I didn't know how. I wished Magda were here, I missed her lively mind. She had left word that she would arrive tomorrow.

Meanwhile, it seemed a good idea to visit the manager of the Keystone Bank. Thanks to Harry Agha I now had $10,000 in an account there, which would provide a plausible excuse.

I switched on the television and surfed for news, On CNN, an anchorwoman with perfect hair was reporting what she clearly thought was a heck of a story.

The crawler at the bottom of the screen said *"Billionaire Publisher drowned."*

Frowning into the camera, she read with studied emphasis:

"Early today, the naked body of publishing mogul Sidney Baxter was found floating near his yacht in Monte Carlo.

Staff on the luxury vessel grew concerned when Mr. Baxter did not appear for breakfast. According to his assistant Leila Cavour, Baxter often swam alone in the early morning. The cause of death is being investigated but foul play is not suspected."

NO FOUL PLAY. Really?

54

Besides Oliver, several other parties were converging on St. Lydia.

First to arrive was the photographer and contract killer Zafi. He was in the same hotel as Oliver.

His orders had been short and sweet – go to St. Lydia and eliminate someone whose identity he would learn on arrival. He left Los Angeles within hours so as to give himself time to recover from jet lag, which could be dangerous in his line of work.

His equipment, including scuba gear and a compressed-air harpoon gun, attracted little attention at Los Angeles airport because he checked the gun and gear as unaccompanied baggage, joking with airline personnel about his fishing trip. They were not very interested. He carried his camera with him.

Arriving at the Frangipani Inn, he checked into his bungalow and was unpacking when there was a knock at the door.

A brown-skinned maid stood there holding an envelope.

He tipped her, and slit it open. Inside was an 8 by 10 photo, and a post-it note stuck on the front with a name and room number. He slipped photo and note back in the envelope and put it away in his briefcase.

Then he unzipped the canvas grip containing his underwater equipment. He examined the harpoon gun, sighting along the barrel, releasing the safety catch and working the mechanism without loading it.

Satisfied, he turned to his camera bag and removed the Hasselblad. He put it up to his eye, focusing at a point across the room.

Unexpectedly, he saw movement. A straw-colored scorpion crouched on the parquet. It was stalking a fat palmetto bug a few inches away with a view to supper.

The photographer smiled. He fetched a glass tumbler from the bathroom and tiptoed across the floor. Coming up behind the scorpion, he inverted the glass and lowered it quickly over the creature, trapping it in a transparent prison. The palmetto bug, safe, waddled away.

The scorpion thrashed furiously, hurling itself at the curved sides of its jail. Outside it could see the photographer's unprotected face as the man leaned in to get a better look. Its venomous tail, arched over its back, struck again and again at the thick glass. Ounce for ounce, the photographer reflected, there could be very few examples of such lethal fury in such a small package. The creature earned his professional respect.

After a while exhaustion compelled the scorpion to stop. It lay inert, crouched under the glass. But the photographer was under no illusions about what would happen if he lifted the glass and set it free. Anyone in range would be rewarded with a dangerous and painful sting.

He considered snatching the glass away and squashing the creature under his shoe but he had seen how fast it moved. That involved risk and this was no time for risks. He was here on business. The last thing he needed was a stupid accident. Leaving the scorpion in its glass prison, he stood up and got on with his work.

55

Quentin Teague was the next to arrive. He traveled light, with no checked baggage. Despite the long journey he arrived in buoyant mood, eager to inspect his new acquisition.

Les Lightfoot, the manager of the Keystone Bank of St. Lydia, was there to meet him, having driven the bank's Jaguar to the airport to meet his new boss. On the way he had taken the Jag through the island's only carwash and removed his squash kit from the back seat.

Lightfoot was a balding Yorkshireman with a slight resemblance to the great cricketer Geoffrey Boycott. He had Boycott's dour seriousness without that athlete's rare power of concentration. He looked like a normal, solid bank manager although he had

worked for an unusually large number of banks – he
somehow lacked charm, and senior management
seemed not to want to have him around for more
than a year or two. He had plotted his career accord-
ingly and usually managed to jump from one job to
the next before he was pushed, often with an
increase in salary. Now at the age of forty he was
overpaid for what he did which, truthfully, was not
much.

Quentin Teague took an instant dislike to him.
As the young entrepreneur climbed out of his plane
with a garment bag in one hand and a briefcase in
the other, he saw a worried-looking man whose pale
cheeks and humourless frown proclaimed the func-
tionary that he was. Men like Lightfoot had refused
to lend Teague money when he was getting started,
even treating him with contempt, so he felt no
warmth towards him.

Well-schooled in City of London etiquette, he
hid his dislike behind a warm smile and an energetic
handshake. He let Lightfoot carry his bag and
followed him to the car.

"What's the plan?" he asked.

"I thought we'd have lunch at a place by the
waterfront. Give you a chance to relax."

Teague pushed his glasses up on his nose. "Do
you usually eat lunch?"

"No."

"Nor do I. Let's get to work."

Lightfoot had been warned about Teague's intense management style, but it was still unnerving to be on the receiving end.

In his office, he retreated behind his large desk. The comfort of his padded leather chair reassured him. Teague parked himself casually on the hard chair reserved for customers. Snapping open his briefcase, he took out some financial statements that had been faxed to him the day before.

He had highlighted some sections in yellow. He proceeded to take Lightfoot through them, line by line. After fifteen minutes, Lightfoot felt like a drip-dry suit that had been put through the wringer, but he managed to find explanations for everything.

Teague seemed satisfied, accepting each response with a noncommittal blink. Lightfoot was relieved. A few areas, including his own expenses, would not bear close scrutiny but Teague seemed to have missed them.

Teague said, "Now let's look at customer deposits."

Lightfoot cleared his throat. "We handle the funds of some pretty wealthy people."

"I know that." Teague sounded impatient. "Give me a list of major depositors."

Lightfoot reached in a drawer and produced a computer-generated sheet of numbers and amounts.

Teague scanned it. "No names?"

"That's right. They are numbered accounts."

"Where are the names?"

"In my desk."

"Let me see them."

"I'm not sure if I can do that."

"What do you mean?"

"When a customer opens a numbered account, his name is known only to me and one other officer. It's a security precaution."

"But I bought the bank."

"I know, but the names can only be shown to a designated officer."

"You don't understand. I own the bank."

Lightfoot wanted to avoid a confrontation. This was a new situation for him. His previous bosses had been content to let the identities of account holders remain secret. It gave them deniability. If there was drug money sitting in the bank, they could always say they knew nothing about it and, if things hit the fan, Lightfoot was there to be sacrificed. Lightfoot understood that; it was what he was paid for. Now Teague wanted to change the rules and Lightfoot was flustered.

"I know it seems odd," he said. "But if a customer suffers loss due to a breach of confidentiality, it's my neck on the block. And there are spies around, believe me. The island is crawling with IRS agents."

That was untrue. In older financial centres like the Bahamas, long a refuge for US flight money, there were 'tourists' in baggy shorts on Uncle Sam's payroll, hanging around Bay Street, snapping photos of suspected customers. That was one reason depositors came to smaller islands like St. Lydia. Its government knew which side its bread was buttered and was very protective of its customer-friendly image. Anyone taking photos outside Keystone Bank was very strongly discouraged.

Teague knew this and so did Lightfoot. Teague eyed the bank manager in silence.

Finally he smiled. "The shareholders held a meeting this morning. They appointed me director and chairman, so I am now an officer. Okay?"

Lightfoot knew better than to push his luck. He reached down and touched a numeric keypad under his desk. A drawer slid out. His hand shook slightly as he gave Teague the folder. "This is the most confidential file in the bank. Not even my secretary has seen it."

There was a list of accounts in Lightfoot's tidy handwriting. Beside the name of each depositor was a password and a date.

Teague spread the two lists on the desk, side by side. By comparing the list of deposits with the list of names, he could see the amount of each depositor's balance. Many were quite small; the average balance was about $10,000.

"Why would anyone have a numbered account, but keep so little money in it?" Teague asked.

"Beats me," said Lightfoot.

"Secrecy?"

Lightfoot shook his head. "They don't get much more secrecy than they would with a conventional account. To reveal a depositor's identity is a criminal offence in St. Lydia law."

"So why?"

"Ego, perhaps. It makes people feel important."

Quentin Teague studied the bigger deposits. Most of the names meant nothing to him, but he soon saw what he was looking for.

The largest single deposit, for just over $400 million, listed a mailing address in Manila. An entity called 'Perez Trust III' was named as the account holder. The names of Ferdinand and Imelda Marcos, Raoul Cerdan Senior and Raoul Cerdan Junior all appeared as authorized signatories. Teague had struck paydirt. He felt a thrill as he read the names. This must be how gold prospectors felt when they saw the glint of a seam.

The St. Lydia attorney who had drawn up the trust, Wolfang de Freitas, was the fifth signatory. The address given for the Cerdans was in Manila. Teague memorized this information, closed the file and handed it to Lightfoot. The manager put it back in the drawer, which he shut and locked.

Teague leaned back in his chair.

"How do you feel about the bank's liquidity?" he asked.

"It's very good," said Lightfoot, surprised.

"Could you withstand a sudden run by depositors?" Teague's smile indicated that the question was hypothetical.

"Depends on the severity. We have $500 million in cash and short-term deposits with other banks."

Teague pulled the balance sheet towards him and tapped it with a finger. "Customer deposits are nearly $600 million; that's more than your entire liquid balance. If they all wanted their money at once, you would be caught short."

"Why on earth would that happen?"

"It's possible."

Lightfoot's voice rose. "It's inconceivable. Local law requires that we maintain a certain ratio of capital to deposits. The ratio here is even stricter than either British or US requirements and, in any case, we pass the test with room to spare."

He knew Teague understood banking liquidity perfectly well. He wondered where the young man was going.

"Let's be cautious," said Teague. "Let's stop paying depositors for a bit."

Lightfoot stared at him in shock. It was the worst possible thing a bank could do. The mere hint of non-payment would spark panic and a rush of withdrawals. Even if the bank survived, it would never again be so attractive to depositors.

"Not for long," said Teague, blinking mildly. "Just for a while. Wouldn't want a run on the bank." He stood up to leave.

"Wait!" Lightfoot' voice rose. "Please think carefully. Our liquidity is fine, you know that. Your proposal is self-destructive. Your whole group would be damaged, not just the bank."

He glared at Teague, trying to fathom this well-dressed young tough. He wanted to be respectful but the best he could manage was a sickly smile on a face as red as a beetroot.

Teague watched him, expressionless. It amused him to propose something outrageous and then let it be watered down by more cautious counsel. Some of his best deals had started out that way.

His first thought had been to simply withdraw $400 million and close the Marcos account for good. Some would call that stealing but Teague had a fine capacity to sail close to the wind and convince himself that it was okay, especially if he was unlikely to be found out. He had thought this through. The Marcos people would probably not make a noise since their legal and moral claims to the money were flimsy in the extreme. They would suck it up and keep quiet. The rest of the world knew where much of the late dictator's money was, but not this particular cache, so secrecy seemed assured.

Then he had second thoughts. The problem was Lightfoot. He did not trust the man an inch, not now and certainly not after Teague fired him, which he would shortly do. To let him stay on, with his loyalty for sale to any nosy journalist, was unthinkable. Gossip in the banking world traveled at the speed of light and this tale of high jinks on a Caribbean island would soon get around. Given the regulatory climate in London and on Wall Street, it would land Teague in hot water for sure.

So he changed his mind. He would be more indirect, use his control of the bank not to steal the money but merely to prevent his competitors from getting their hands on it. He had another plan for later, after all the fuss had died down, but it was not something to be shared with the agitated bank manager.

"Let's do this," he said. "Any withdrawal under ten grand, go ahead, no problem. Anything bigger, call me first."

Lightfoot scowled. Despite the compromise, he had just been stripped of his authority.

"One last thing," said Teague.

"What?"

"No mistakes. This will be worth your while, trust me. But one hint of independent action by you, and you're dead. I'll start by taking a close look at those expenses of yours."

Lightfoot stayed silent.

"Is that clear?"

"Yes."

"That's my boy."

RAOUL CERDAN, SON OF PRESIDENT MARCOS' personal attorney, was also on his way to St. Lydia. News of Sidney Baxter's death had not yet filtered through to him as his plane approached the island. So, when he landed in St. Lydia at dusk and walked through the little airport, he was surprised to be met by a woman.

56

Can I get you a drink, Sir?"

It was dusk and I was lounging on a rattan sofa in the lobby of the Banana Grove Hotel in Georgetown, waiting for Magda to arrive. She was staying there because my own hotel was full.

I liked the place. The lobby was open to the sky – a mellow courtyard with the scent of hibiscus hanging in the warm air. She had insisted she didn't want to be met at the airport which was fine with me.

The cocktail waiter was a young islander in white levis and flowered shirt, a diamond in one ear. His badge said "Val."

"Rum Collins please, Val."

I enjoyed my drink for a few minutes. Then my serenity was shattered by some surprise visitors.

The first was Leila, my new best pal from Monte Carlo.

She descended the broad staircase from the upper of two floors – no hotel on St. Lydia is taller than the tops of the surrounding palms. She looked gorgeous in a lime-green cocktail dress and diamonds, probably real. She seemed to be looking around for someone. Instinct made me grab a magazine from the coffee table and hide behind it.

It wasn't hard to guess why she was here. Actually I could think of 400 million reasons. I didn't know whether to be annoyed or amused. I had expected she would still be in Monaco, mourning – outwardly – the passing of a beloved boss, but here she was, sniffing round the honey pot with the billionaires.

She was greeted moments later by two men, both of whom I knew. The first was my boss Carlton Tisch, short and thin with iron-grey curls, looking as if he spent a lot of time in the sun. Carlton was the last person I expected to see on St. Lydia. He was wearing a white tropical suit that needed pressing. His tie was loose and the shirt collar unbuttoned, as if the outfit had just undergone a substantial journey. He carried a briefcase and looked cross as usual.

The other man was the same height but with a

broader chest and long arms. His open-necked shirt and khakis were vaguely military, making him look like an ageing soldier of fortune. There was something rough about him – an animal quality that made him look simian and tough; the word louche came to mind. This was Carlton's friend, Kon Feaver.

The waiter brought my drink. I fished the paper parasol out of the glass and put it back on his tray with a tip.

"What are those two doing here?"

The waiter looked at me. "No idea mon."

TISCH AND FEAVER WENT UPSTAIRS. Leila slipped away. I looked at my watch. Magda was due to arrive in twenty minutes.

I went and sat at the bar, thinking things over. It would be better not to be seen with Magda by these people. I drained my Rum Collins. As I left the bar, I almost bumped into Kon Feaver.

"Steady, Oliver!"

"Sorry, Kon."

"Not your fault." The accent was Israeli. The voice was calm, making me feel clumsy. We eyed each other for a second. He smiled. I left the Banana Grove Hotel immediately. My meeting with Magda would have to wait.

57

Mr. Cerdan?"

Raoul blinked. "I expected a man."

"Life is full of surprises." Leila ushered him into the chauffeur-driven Lincoln she had rented for the occasion. The driver took Raoul's bag.

Raoul and Leila sized each other up.

She saw a plump young Filipino whose sulky face was consistent with being spoiled by women, from his nurse and his mother to his wife and mistresses. She also saw a valuable meal ticket.

He saw a dark-haired woman whose expensive dress and jewellery were a bit over the top in an island setting.

She returned his stare, dollar for dollar. Tired as

he was after his journey, he was already imagining making love to her.

They sat in the back of the Ford, their thighs nearly touching.

"Why am I here?" he asked.

"I think you know," she said.

"Remind me."

"You have some banking matters to attend to."

"Can you be more specific?"

"It involves closing certain accounts."

He frowned. "I have no idea who you are."

"Doesn't matter."

"I think it does."

"I am charged with executing the wishes of the late Ara Kalestian."

"Which are?"

"To close the account at Keystone Bank."

"Where are we going now?"

"To your hotel. You can rest after your journey."

They drove in silence.

"What about my arrangement with Kalestian?" asked Raoul.

"It will be honored."

"How do I know I can trust you?"

"Let me explain," she said with a note of exasperation, "We'll go to the bank tomorrow. We shall close the accounts. We'll use the proceeds to make two bank transfers. Not one, two. One of those will be for your commission. You can have cash or, if you prefer, a certified check."

"And that's it?"

"That's it. You can't be cheated, you are in control the whole way. Good?"

Raoul thought some more. Things were moving alarmingly fast. But apparently, within twenty-four hours he would be released from his obligations, the worrying would be over and he would also be a great deal richer.

There were some practical issues. Things had changed in the Philippines. It was less acceptable now to be rich and pro-Marcos. It might be wise to stay away for a while. But he could live with that. Madrid was nice at this time of year.

"One question," he said.

"Yes?"

"Are you free for dinner?"

"Of course."

58

L eila waited as Raoul checked in, unaware that she herself was being watched.

Magda, who had just arrived, was applying lipstick using a small mirror. It was something she was normally too fastidious to do in public but, using the mirror, she could observe Leila clearly.

Once she was sure of what she had seen, she went to a house phone and called Oliver's room. Receiving no answer, she left a message on his voicemail.

When she finished, Leila was still in the lobby, standing at a counter writing a postcard. Magda strolled over and stood next to her.

As Leila concentrated on her postcard, Magda pushed her purse sideways until it was next to Leila's elbow. Moments later the inevitable happened. Leila nudged the purse which fell to the floor, sending money, cosmetics and other small items rolling across the marble floor.

Full of apologies, Leila fell to her knees and helped Magda recapture the objects and shovel them back in the purse. Equally polite, Magda protested that she herself was to blame. As they knelt on the cool tile, the women's eyes met and both smiled.

"Too much stuff," said Magda.

"Tell me about it," said Leila.

"I was about to grab some coffee. Want to join me?"

Leila looked indecisive, consulted her watch and smiled. "Upstairs in my suite?

"Perfect."

IN MY ROOM, I played Magda's message. With Leila and Cerdan both here, things were heating up. Alarm bells went off. If I didn't speak to the young Filipino pretty soon, I could wind up at the back of a crowded field with no hope of making up lost ground.

I grabbed pen and paper. I'm no lawyer but, like most accountants, I've read enough legal stuff that I can fake the jargon pretty well. I scribbled out a

Power of Attorney for Cerdan to sign, adding some wrinkles of my own. I then wrote a very large check using my clean new Keystone Bank check book.

At the front desk, pleading urgency, I got the document typed while I waited. Then I called Cerdan and, lying fluently, introduced myself as a lawyer for the late Sidney Baxter. I asked to meet in the bar.

Our meeting didn't start well. I had assumed that, because Cerdan spoke good English, he would be communicative. But he was taciturn and surly.

He did seem to accept my status as Baxter's representative. But he seemed to think that the death of Ara Kalestian released him from his gambling debts, and that he was now a free agent. I needed to disabuse him.

"We need you to sign over the Marcos money."

His face split in a sneer. "Give me a reason."

"You owe more than a million dollars in gambling debts."

"Those were owed to Kalestian. He's dead."

"Yes but his death changes nothing. The IOUs were owed to the Excelsior. Mr. Baxter bought the IOUs from the hotel and his estate now owns them."

Cerdan scowled. "Baxter's girl will give me a better deal."

"Miss Cavour has no legal authority." I produced the POA from my briefcase. "Our lawyers prepared this. If you sign a power of attorney transferring the Marcos funds to a designated account, we will cancel your debts. Only then will you be free and clear."

He read the paper suspiciously. I had used plenty of long words and, in the best legal tradition, made the syntax as awkward as possible.

"This transfer is made out to you personally, not to Baxter," he complained.

"A legal necessity," I said shortly. "To avoid probate, since both Kalestian and Baxter are dead."

I held my breath. It was nonsense, of course. But Cerdan heard the dreaded word probate which, as everyone knows, involves major delays, freezing assets for months or even years. He still seemed unconvinced, so I decided to play my trump card. I produced the check.

"One last thing. Mr. Baxter really appreciated your help, so before he died, he ordered that your services be properly recognized. This is a check for $20 million, dated tomorrow. It's drawn on the account into which you will transfer the funds."

It did the trick. He signed like a lamb and I left, clutching the executed authority. I left him sitting in the dimly lit bar with a drink, studying the check.

I wondered how soon he would hit Leila up for a better offer.

· · ·

THE NEXT MORNING, I went to see de Freitas, the attorney who was Harry Agha's cousin. His office was in a quiet turning off Front Street, St. Lydia's business centre full of banks and lawyers. Flowering creeper climbed the walls of a pink-roofed cottage. A bicycle with a wicker shopping basket leaned against the wall.

A brass nameplate said:

Wolfang Doss de Freitas, Solicitor.

Member, St. Lydia Bar.

The door was open, so I walked in.

"Hi, Mr Steele." The pretty secretary had a big smile and an island accent.

The modern office belied the building's rustic exterior. Printers hummed. Screens flickered. One printer pumped out pages of text; another, three-across labels. A dark-skinned man emerged from an office next door.

"Mr de Freitas?"

"Wolfang, please."

About forty, brown as a berry with white teeth in a humorous face. He reminded me of photos I had seen of Gurkha troops from Nepal, hard and tough. Straight black hair glistened with some kind of gel.

"Your cousin Harry sends his regards," I said.

"How is the old devil?"

"He's fine. So's his Rolls Royce."

Wolfang laughed. "He's incorrigible. No fool though."

"Your office looks very productive."

"Amazing what computers can do, eh? This small building is the headquarters for more than five hundred corporations."

"Must take a lot of human input."

"Not really. Dawn here is my only employee. For many clients, we are their billing department, corporate office, you name it."

"Transfer Pricing?"

"For goods that never come here physically? Of course. They are purchased at one price and sold onward at a higher price with the difference settling here on this tax-free island."

"Impressive."

He grinned. "Come in. A drink?"

His office was a comfortable jumble after the efficiency outside. He waved me to an easy chair.

"How can I help?"

"A few years ago, somebody drew up a trust for the Marcos family."

De Freitas said nothing.

"My questions are about that."

"As long as you don't wish me to breach confidentiality."

So this was the man who had set up the Marcos

Trust. St. Lydia was a tiny island with few lawyers, so no great surprise.

"Do you know Raoul Cerdan?"

"No comment."

"Do you deny that you know him?"

"No comment."

I liked the look of de Freitas, so I charged ahead anyway. I told him most of the story, stressing that the funds represented embezzlement by persons in high office. When I finished, he thought for a minute.

"What is it you want?"

"I want to stop those funds falling into bad hands."

de Freitas shook his head. "You seem a decent person and your motives are good but I am not obliged to help you."

I shrugged my shoulders. "You know what's going on. I want to stop Cerdan from signing away that money, at least until I know it's going to the rightful owners, the people of the Philippines."

He thought for a minute.

"Here's a suggestion. Under St. Lydia law, you could petition the court for something called an administrative audit. That would take several weeks and, meanwhile, the account would be frozen. That would buy you time."

"Can you help me do that?"

"Yes, but there are some issues I need to research."

"What issues?"

"Points of law."

"When will you know?"

"Call me tomorrow, around one o'clock."

That was as far as I could get him to go. When I left, he shook my hand and looked me in the eye. That usually means the speaker is sincere but sometimes it just means he's lying through his teeth and trying to hide the fact.

59

Outside, I blinked in the sun. It was 11:30. Not much to do until I spoke to de Freitas next day.

Pointless to fret, I was in the Caribbean. Which meant one thing – the beach.

My mini-moke was parked where I left it, the air shimmering above its radiator. I studied the map in the glove box.

St. Lydia's beaches are strung out along its western coastline and separated by several huge granite outcrops. In the guidebook, Crescent Beach caught my eye – described as 'a mile-long curve of yellow sand, usually deserted, with a coral reef offshore, great for snorkeling.'

I bought a ham roll at a kiosk, and set out. I followed the coast road north, keeping the ocean on my left until the road swung inland past Cathedral Point, a great volcanic rock a mile wide that thrust up from the seabed millions of years ago.

Traffic was light. Two hundred yards back, a Chevy Beretta in rent-a-car white was following me. I kept my eye on it. I try not to be paranoid, but you never know. A wooden sign said 'Crescent Beach, 2 miles.' Leaving the road, I bumped along a jungle trail. In the mirror I saw the Beretta whiz by and disappear and I relaxed.

The track led through woods in a natural tunnel of foliage. Finally, I reached a clearing with a picnic table, and then the beach.

I donned a swimsuit and headed seaward carrying goggles and towel.

As advertised, I had the beach to myself. White-caps marked the reef, 70 yards out. I waded into the warm water and swam out to sea.

Underwater visibility was amazing – blue-green parrotfish jostled for space with lugubrious bass and yellow angelfish. A flat stingray rose up from its place on the ocean floor, shedding sand and flapped away on urgent business.

Back on land, I ate my sandwich and gazed out to sea. There was movement on the surface of the water and a dark shadow flickered and vanished, then reappeared, breaking the surface close to shore.

Out of the waves came a man in a scarlet bathing

suit with a buoyancy vest and a steel tank on his back. He had a harpoon gun in one hand and a watertight camera in the other. He set the camera down on the sand and turned towards me, smiling. I could not see his face because the mask covered his eyes and nose but he had white teeth and a good tan.

We were alone, just the two of us.

"Nice diving weather," I said.

"Almost perfect."

"Have you dived many places?" I asked, to make conversation.

"Thailand, Borneo. The Great Barrier Reef of course."

He pushed his mask up. It was the photographer Zafi.

He shrugged and said, "Sorry."

"I guess I picked the wrong beach."

"I would have found you anyway."

"So now what?" I asked.

"I think you know."

The harpoon gun was raised and ready. Ten feet separated us. It could have been ten miles for all the opportunity it offered. His brown eyes, which had roamed around the beach came to rest on my face. To all intents and purposes I was dead.

60

Tell me a couple of things," I said.

"I'll try. I really don't know very much."

"You are going to kill me and you don't know why?" I asked. I tried to inject some scorn but I was trembling slightly.

"It's my job."

"Just business?"

He nodded. "A service performed for a fee." He undid the straps across his chest and let the tank slip down onto the sand.

"Who are you working for, now that Baxter is dead?"

A second shadow materialized in the water and took human form as its owner stood up in the shallows. Zafi was facing me with his back to the ocean and was not aware of the newcomer.

A concert of sound reached my ears – the breeze, the lapping of waves, the roar of bigger waves out by the reef – but no sudden report.

But Zafi's body lurched as if shoved from behind and his hands flew back, trying to scratch an inaccessible place in the small of his back. A bloody red bump appeared on his chest where he had undone the harness. It was the tip of a harpoon. He lurched and fell to his knees, arms scrabbling.

The bow-legged figure of Kon Feaver waded ashore.

"Thanks," I said.

"Thought you might need some help."

He ignored Zafi who had fallen forward on the sand, eyes glazing.

"Should we do something?" I asked.

"Like what?"

"Help him."

"He's a piece of dirt. He'll be dead in a minute."

"It seems a bit cold-blooded."

The Israeli looked at me quizzically. "He was going to do you the same favour."

He slapped me on the back. "Help me drag him into the bushes."

We got Zafi up the beach and into the undergrowth. Feaver scooped a shallow hole in the earth and leaves and we tipped the body in, along with his gear, and more or less covered it up.

"That should do for a while," said Feaver. There was a slight mound in the leaves, as well as two parallel tracks left by the body's heels as we dragged it along. He kicked and scuffed the marks to make them less obvious. "This place is pretty remote. In a month, when the tourist season really gets going, someone will find him."

"Then what?"

Kon shrugged. "Who cares? We'll be long gone. Speaking of which, I could use a ride back to my car which is over by the next beach – I had quite a long swim."

I guided the mini-moke through the woods and back to the main road. I looked across at Feaver who seemed unconcerned.

"I've been wondering," I said. "Who was Zafi's second employer? After Baxter died, I mean."

"I guess we'll never find out."

But he looked as if he knew more than he wanted to say.

IN THE MIDDLE of the night, the phone rang. It was Magda.

"Want to hear some pillow talk?"

"It's three in the morning."

"This is important."

"It had better be."

"Carlton Tisch has talked the Filipino into going to the bank with him."

I had expected Carlton to take a hand in the game, so I was not surprised.

"I thought Leila had enticed Cerdan into her corner."

"She thought so too," said Magda. "She's livid."

"What happened?"

"She met Cerdan at the airport and took him under her wing. Then you had your chat with Cerdan. But afterwards, she collared him again. Over an intimate dinner, she persuaded him to stick with Baxter's original plan. It involved going to the bank next day – this morning – and closing the bank account. She would take most of the money, with Cerdan getting a hefty finder's fee."

"Enough to better my offer."

"But there's more. Just as they were finishing dinner and Leila was getting ready to go upstairs with Raoul and seal things with a kiss, in walks Carlton with Kon Feaver and they take Cerdan aside for a chat."

"Kon can be quite persuasive."

"I guess so. When Cerdan comes back to the table, the deal is off."

"Carlton offered him more money?"

"Presumably. Leila thinks Carlton and Kon also promised to hand Cerdan his cojones on a plate if he didn't play ball. Cerdan's reserves of courage are no match for that type of persuasion."

"And Leila had no answer for that?"

"Well, that's an odd thing. Apparently she has a hired gun of her own on the island."

I pricked up my ears. "Does this gun have a name?"

"He probably does but I don't know it. She confronted Tisch and Feaver and said as much to them but they just laughed, so her threat fell flat. After they left, she tried to contact her man but she couldn't reach him."

"I think I know why." I thought of the fresh grave out at the beach.

This was additional proof of who ordered the killing of Ara Kalestian because, if the photographer was working for Leila, she must have inherited him from Sidney Baxter. That proved that Baxter had ordered Kalestian's death. I knew now how Baxter had drowned, given that Leila was an expert scuba diver.

"What happens next?" I asked.

"Tisch, Feaver and Cerdan have an appointment at the bank at 9.30am, that's in six hours' time."

"You were right to call me in the middle of the night."

"I thought so."

I recalled the Power of Attorney with Raoul Cerdan's signature on it, now lying on my desk. Raoul did not score very well for loyalty. I would have to nip in and see the bank manager early, before he saw Tisch. Magda must have read my thoughts because she said, "The bank opens at nine. That gives you time."

I was so busy planning to forestall Tisch that I forget to ask how she coaxed so much information out of Leila.

61

W hen I walked into the bank at 9:01, I was feeling good. Things were going according to plan. The two men responsible for killing Kalestian were both dead and I would shortly have my hands on more money than I had ever controlled in my life. At which time I would play God and dispose of it in a righteous way.

Lightfoot, the bank manager, came out and shook my hand but he avoided looking me in the eye. I sensed something amiss. In his office, he leaned back in his chair. I opened my briefcase and handed him the order from Cerdan.

I said, "I'd like to close the account and draw three cashiers' checks. I assume that's convenient?"

He glanced at the order and handed it back.

"The account is closed."

"Closed?"

"There are no remaining funds. In accordance with bank policy, the account is cancelled."

I should have been surprised, but, deep down, I was not. Too many players milling about for something not to go wrong.

"Who closed it?"

"I can't tell you, you have no standing."

"You could tell me anyway," I said. He shook his head.

I was not going to grovel. The game was over.

I stood up. Lightfoot seemed reluctant to leave it at that.

"Everything was done properly, old man."

"Properly?"

"In accordance with banking rules."

"Which banking rules are those?"

"The St. Lydia Finance Act."

"Oh, right."

I tried to keep the disappointment out of my voice. I was baffled now as to who had the money. Based on what Magda told me in the small hours, I assumed it was Carlton Tisch but, on my way out of the bank, I passed Carlton going in. If the account was closed, why was he only now arriving?

With him were Kon Feaver and overweight Raoul Cerdan in a lot of gold jewelry. He avoided my eye too.

Carlton apparently still thought Cerdan was the key to a payoff. But as he was about to learn, that key no longer fitted the lock. I would like to have been a fly on the wall when he and Raoul got the bad news and started in on each other.

As Carlton passed within a foot of me, I leaned towards him. "Don't count your chickens." He threw me a look of measured malice.

But if Carlton didn't scoop the pool, who did? For a brief while I had fancied my own chances. Then when I saw Leila Cavour stepping into Sidney Baxter's shoes, I was sure she would be the winner. Later I was convinced that Tisch had intimidated Cerdan into joining him. One by one, all the obvious answers proved to be wrong. So where did things stand?

Not until I was in the mini-moke and driving back to the hotel did a thought strike me. I pictured the flat, bespectacled face of the Hon. Quentin Teague, the new owner of Keystone Bank. Who was best positioned to trump Tisch's ace? Who better than the banker himself?

62

On the private beach of the Frangipani Resort, deck chairs were set up under colored umbrellas. A few guests were already out there, enjoying an iced tea or something stronger.

One patch of sand was occupied by three people I recognized.

Quentin Teague, workaholic was apparently off duty today. In dark glasses and natty tartan shorts, he sat like a pasha while Leila Cavour, topless as was her wont, rubbed oil on his chest. It looked as if Leila might have changed horses again – first Baxter, then me, then Cerdan, and now the British banker.

I was processing this idea when the third member rolled over and sat up. It was Magda, also topless and apparently in need of oiling, because she beckoned to Leila who hastened to do the honors.

Sitting on a beach towel with Leila rubbing her back, Magda spotted me and waved. I went over.

"Morning all," I said.

Teague nodded at me. "Do you know my new associate, Miss Leila Cavour?"

"We've met."

"Miss Cavour is joining Keystone Holdings as Director of Hospitality Services. It's a new position." Behind the stolid face, a sense of humor?

"I'm sure she'll be a great success."

"No doubt."

"I suppose congratulations about the Marcos trust are in order too," I said. He raised his eyebrows.

"The money."

He still said nothing. I said, "I just came from the bank. I think you were there before me."

He nodded. "Yes, I was."

"Now that you've won the Game, what will you do with the funds?"

He did not exactly seem elated. I had expected that outwitting the opposition would put him in a good mood but clearly there was something on his mind.

"How about a swim?" he said.

We walked to the edge of the water. "Race you to that raft," he said.

He was a good swimmer, cleaving his way through the sea with a strong crawl before pulling himself up on the raft. I climbed up after him and we lay in the sun, looking back to shore. Magda had rolled over, the back done, and was receiving frontal attention.

"They make a nice couple," observed Teague.

"Yes, they do."

After a moment's silence, he looked over at me.

"It wasn't me."

"Sorry?"

"I didn't get the money. Must be someone else."

I looked blank.

"I thought it was you, actually," he said.

"Not guilty. But if you knew someone was going to withdraw the funds, why didn't you freeze the account? "

"I thought about it, believe me. But something came up."

"What?"

"Something most people wouldn't understand. I had a call yesterday from Sir Percy Martin, the Political Resident. He's the Queen's representative here on St. Lydia, a sort of ambassador."

"And?"

"He plays golf with my father."

"Did he invite you for sherry?"

"Sherry and a chat. The sherry was fine, the chat was the problem."

"Let me guess. He threatened to report you for not playing cricket with a straight bat."

"Something like that. There's an issue between my father and me concerning the family home, Hambleden Castle: who will get it when he dies."

"Not you?"

"Probably, but not certainly. Under the will of the first baron, two hundred years ago, the castle descends through the male line. I am the eldest son, so normally I would inherit."

"Which is something you want?"

"Yes. The castle is important to me."

"Is it valuable?"

"Oh, it's worth a lot. The Rembrandts alone are worth £50 million. But its value to me is sentimental. I want it."

"Won't you inherit automatically?"

"My father can designate any male heir he wishes. I have two younger brothers. It could go to either of them."

"And would, if he were really annoyed at you?"

"He already disapproves strongly of my aggressive business methods."

"And a negative word from Sir Percy could tip the scales?"

"Exactly. And now Keystone's manager, the

unspeakable Lightfoot, has spun him some absurd tale about me wanting to violate local banking laws. Sir Percy, who is a nice old bird but very conservative, read me a lecture about how important it was to preserve St. Lydia's good name."

"Is he right?"

"Well it's important to St. Lydia. Without the banking, this island is just a second-tier cruise stopover with bad roads."

"He threatened to report you to your father?"

"Yes."

"So you've pulled out of the Game, writing off $2 million and a lot of time and effort."

He shrugged. "It's not a complete waste. The bank will come in useful. The manager's a jerk but I'll fire him."

"And Leila."

"She's making herself useful already."

All this was interesting but I still had a big question.

"Who did get the money?"

"I was about to ask you."

"I'm out of ideas. You can find out, can't you?"

"Sure. But let's see if we can work it out. I guess the winner came up with a better plan than you. How were you going to get Lightfoot to release the money?"

"My plan was to work with de Freitas, the attorney who drafted the trust."

Teague nodded. "Good thinking. What happened?"

"He told me yesterday that he would think about it. But I suspect he already had another client with the same goal in mind. I thought he meant Carlton Tisch."

"But it wasn't Tisch. Let's see, de Freitas, what kind of name is that? Portuguese?"

"Goanese, perhaps. He's dark skinned."

"Goa, yes. Not many places speak Portuguese. There's Brazil."

"Or Macau."

Teague snapped his fingers. "That's it."

"What?"

"Macau. Think about it, where's Macau?"

"It's off the coast of China," I said. "Two hours from Hong Kong by hovercraft."

"And who comes from Hong Kong?"

The penny dropped. "Louise Chang. But what's the connection?"

"It doesn't matter. That's the gal. That's your winner."

63

The message light was blinking in my hotel room. The operator gave me a 'phone number but no name. I didn't really need one.

"Hello?" The hollow intonation was distinctive.

"Dr Chang?"

"Hi, Mr Steele."

"You seem to be a step ahead of the rest of us."

There was a silence. Then, "Why not come and see me. We can have a cup of tea."

"Where are you?"

"I am on Martinique. I was on St. Lydia for a few hours but I thought it best to leave yesterday. If you catch the afternoon flight and go to Hotel Le Cap Est, you'll find me in the lounge."

"I can do that. I'm pretty much finished here."

"Yes you are," said Louise Chang. "Just one thing."

"What?"

"Don't let the Martinique cab drivers cheat you. Agree a price in advance before they drive you in from the airport."

"Yes, ma'am."

I packed my belongings and carried my bag out to the lobby. As I was getting into my taxi, white-suited Carlton Tisch accosted me. He was literally shaking, his thin face taut.

"I want to talk to you," he gritted.

"Not a good time – in a bit of a rush," I apologized over my shoulder and waved the cab to move ahead. When I looked back he was in the middle of the road, shaking his fist. Talk about a sore loser.

IN MARTINIQUE, cab drivers go about their business with a fatalism not uncommon in the Caribbean and are inclined to be surly. Mine was not made any happier by our negotiation regarding the fare. He maintained silence during the journey.

Hotel le Cap Est was expensively elegant, like its guest, Louise Chang. On my way to the lounge, I passed the dining room which looked like a serious place. I promised myself a visit, not this time perhaps but one day.

Dr. Chang sat on a sofa, looking frail and non-threatening. She motioned me to join her.

"Sitting here, I was recalling the financier Meyer Lansky, banker to your American 'mob,' whose office was the lobby of a Miami Beach hotel."

"How did you persuade de Freitas to fall in with your plans? Did you pay him?"

"Not with money."

"Meaning?"

"Mr. de Freitas' family are Portuguese-Indian merchants, originally from Goa, now in Macau. Conditions in Macau are uncertain – it's now a Special Administrative Region of the Chinese Republic."

"Did you offer to help his family?"

She nodded. "Under the new regime it can be better to be Chinese than Portuguese."

"Or to have Chinese friends?"

"One has some influence."

I got the point but I still didn't understand how she had got the account at Keystone cleaned out so swiftly, so I asked her.

"It wasn't difficult."

"How come?"

"De Freitas was not entirely frank with you."

"I gather that."

"Do you know what a Protector is?"

That rang a bell. I remembered Victor Aronson

explaining trusts to me in London. The Protector was the person who could dismiss the trustee.

"Who is the Protector in this trust?"

"The attorney, de Freitas, was the Protector."

"How can that be? Surely the Marcos people knew that they were giving great power to an outsider?"

"I guess they didn't read the small print. Many clients don't, they just sign at the bottom. Especially if their lawyer tells them it's okay."

"Why would de Freitas do that?"

"Who knows? He has quite a subtle mind."

I was at a loss for words. Everyone had forgotten about the concept of the Protector except the woman sitting opposite me. Louise Chang had out-thought all her competitors and left them in the dust.

"How did you find out who the Protector was?"

"I asked him," she said simply.

She described how she had made things work. All that was necessary was to get a letter from de Freitas in his capacity as the Protector, dismissing the previous Trustee, a Philippine bank, and appointing her trustee in its place. From then on, she had power over the trust and its money. I now understood why de Freitas had put me off. He was already working for Louise Chang.

I finished my drink. "Well, you won. How will you spend the money?"

"Apply it would be a better word," she said. "I do not need any more for myself.

I waited but that was all she had to say. It was time to leave. She reached in her purse and brought out a slip of paper.

"This is for you." It was a check for $100,000, drawn on Chang Shipping's account at the Belize City branch of the Royal Bank of Canada.

"For your trouble," she said. "Thank you."

I had a brief debate with myself about whether accepting it would compromise my principles but I could not think of any particular principle that had been compromised so I put it in my pocket.

EPILOGUE

Shortly after my meeting with Louise Chang on Martinique, an anonymous donor gave $400 million to a fund for the victims of Philippine atrocities, according to the New York Times.

I never heard any more about the extraction of $400 million from a small private bank on St. Lydia.

THE END

More reading

Here are some more Kon Feaver and Oliver Steele thrillers. You can order from any bookstore or go to the author's website: **www.grahamtempest.com** and order from there.

CASINO CARIBBEAN

Steele and Kon Feaver are sent to Antigua to discourage a drug dealer turned internet casino owner who is terrorising an elderly Florida bettor.

CASINO DE FRANCE

Steele and Feaver are sent to Paris to track down a nuclear terrorist who is threatening the city.

CASINO HAVANA

Steele flies to Cuba to rescue Feaver, who has been imprisoned for smuggling refugees to the Florida Keys.

FEAVER PITCH

A friend of Kon and Oliver is brutally murdered in his flat in Miami. A clue to the killer's identity is a crude star-shaped mark scrawled by the victim in his own blood.

JOBURG STEELE

Steele and Feaver fly to South Africa to trace fifty million stolen dollars. The crooked businessmen who blackmailed one government minister and murdered another are waiting for them.

CASINO QADDAFI

Steele traces missing millions to Libya, a place of lethal anarchy after Qaddafi's assassination, battling the slain dictator's murderous henchmen.

ACKNOWLEDGMENTS

Many thanks to Raficq Abdulla, Patricia Cole and Mike Dinkins who read the manuscript of Casino Excelsior and whose advice improved the book in many ways.

Also to editor Sue Berry and cover designer Stuart Bache.

COPYRIGHT

First published in 2012. This edition published in 2026.

Copyright 2026 by Jeremy Stone. All rights reserved.

Graham Tempest is a British-American author who divides his time between Oxfordshire and Florida

www.GrahamTempest.com